BADLAND

DOMINIC R. DANIELS
&
RON DELEON

ISBN: 0692396373
ISBN 13: 9780692396377

Dedicated to
Phil & Mary Daniels

<u>New Books Coming in 2015 (Fiction)</u>
Underground Society 2: Code of Honor (Book 2) Co-Author
The Mystic Journey of Doctor Xoctarius (Book 3) Co-Author

<u>Other Books by Raynaldo D. Deleon II</u>

Underground Society (Book 1) Co-Author

<u>New Books Coming in 2015 (Fiction)</u>

Underground Society 2: Code of Honor (Book 2) Co-Author

FOREWORD

"Badland was originally titled *Slash N' Shop*, about a happily married woman who shops late at night, only to be the unwilling prey of a dangerous deranged ex-military soldier, suffering the mental problems of the War in Iraq and Afghanistan...When I pitched it to Dominic, he liked the idea and we worked on the original screenplay, but it evolved over time to be called *Chop Shop* and later *Badland*, with a brand new story. Now it takes place in the wilderness of California, where four young women are being hunted by a deranged military soldier, who suffers from combat shock...This story was inspired by *Buddy Giovinazzo's Combat Shock*, *Neil Marshall's The Descent*, *The Running Man* and *The Hunger Games*, for so long we as an audience are getting tired of the same horror film clichés and remakes of horror film clichés, so we as emerging writers decided it was time to create something new...The version your about to read is the completed draft...Hopefully if this story transforms into a feature film, it will be different from the book, as most book-turned-films do...We hope you enjoy this female-driven horror story, as much as we(the storytellers do)...Now get ready to be hunted in the California's BADLAND..."

- Raynaldo "Ron" D. DeLeon II (Co-Creator of Badland)

"We hope you enjoy our little grind house story and have one hell of a good time reading it!"

- Dominic R. Daniels (Co-Creator of Badland)

FADE IN:

EXT. LARGE WEED FIELD - NIGHT

A TOW TRUCK DRIVER, 50s, runs desperately away in terror from an unknown figure. He has gunshot wounds through the arm and shoulder.

He hides within the bushes while bleeding to death.

> TOW TRUCK DRIVER
> Help! Somebody help me!

An UNKNOWN FIGURE, wearing hunting fatigues and a mask, pulls out his hunting bow and arrow -- he shoots.

The tow truck driver continues to run.

An arrow pierces right through the back of his head with the arrow tip goes out on center of his skull, like a unicorn with a single horn.

The tow truck driver gags within seconds and falls down dead with the arrow still stuck through his head.

The unknown figure walks to the tow truck driver. He drags the victim by pulling his hair and slits his throat with his hunting knife, decapitating him.

FADE OUT.

FADE IN:

INT. ELEMENTARY SCHOOL CLASSROOM - DAY

JENNIFER SANDERSON, late 20s, sweet and innocent young school teacher with a heart of gold.

She _reads_ "The Cat and the Mice" by Aesop to a group of young second graders.

> JENNIFER
> There was once a house overrun by mice. A cat heard of this, and said to herself, "That's the place for me," and off she went and took up her quarters in the house, and caught the mice one by one and ate them.

She turns the page while the children are listening.

> JENNIFER
> At last the mice could stand it no longer, and they determined to take to their holes and stay there. By and by a mouse peeped out and saw the cat hanging there and said.

She turns the final page while the children are listening.

JENNIFER
"You're very cleaver, madam, no doubt.

But you may turn yourself into a bag of meal hanging there, if you like, yet you won't catch us coming anywhere near you".

TOBY, one of the children raises his hand.

TOBY
What does that mean Mrs. Sanderson?

JENNIFER
It means, Toby, that if you think with your head, you can get out of situations in which someone may try to hurt you. Using your wits is sometimes better than trying to fight your way out of it.

RING!

The clock hits three o'clock and the bell rings. The children begin to pack up their bags.

JENNIFER
Okay everybody -- don't forget to do your assignments tonight. I want you all to do well on the quiz tomorrow. Whoever gets the best grades gets no homework for the weekend and we all go for a class picnic at the park.

The children cheer in joy.

Jennifer smiles at the kids.

JENNIFER
Goodbye guys, see you tomorrow.

The children leave the room.

EXT. EAST LOS ANGELES - DAY

Jennifer walks in the dilapidated city of East Los Angeles with a bag of groceries. She enters her apartment building, where kids are playing out on the streets and a couple of residents smoking and talking on the stoop.

INT. APARTMENT BUILDING - DAY

The apartment building is an old rundown 1960s apartment complex. Jennifer goes up the stairs, through the hallway on the second floor and enters her apartment.

INT. JENNIFER'S APARTMENT - DAY

Jennifer unlocks the door to her apartment, walks in, locks the door, goes into the kitchen_._

INT. KITCHEN - CONTINUOUS

She puts the items on the counter top.

The land line phone rings.

Jennifer picks up her phone.

JENNIFER
Hello?

MALE DOCTOR (V.O.)
Hello, may I speak to Jennifer Sanderson?

JENNIFER
Who is this?

MALE DOCTOR (V.O.)
This is Doctor Davidson, calling from Saint Mary's Hospital in Moreno Valley.

JENNIFER
This is Mrs. Sanderson speaking. What's this call regarding about?

DOCTOR DAVIDSON (V.O.)
Mrs. Sanderson, we have been caring for your mother here for the past few weeks. I am sorry to inform you the bad news... your mother has ovarian cancer.

Jennifer is shocked at the news.

JENNIFER
My God... how long does she have?

DOCTOR DAVIDSON (V.O.)
We don't know, probably a week or two. She's not doing well. She wanted us to call you to request that you come see her before she passes.

JENNIFER
I will be there in about a couple of days. Thank you doctor.

Jennifer hangs up the phone. She is silent for a few moments... until, she softly cries.

A memorial photo of Jennifer's father and younger sister is displayed on the counter -- with the words, "Matthew Clarke, 1950-2011" and "Nicole Clarke, 1992-2011". Her maiden name is Clarke.

INT. APARTMENT - DAY

Jennifer's husband BRUCE SANDERSON, 36, an overworked, stressed, emotionally tired, angry and bitter lawyer, arrives in the apartment. He just lost another case with one of his clients. He is dressed in a business suit and tie.

Bruce sighs.

INT. KITCHEN - DAY

Jennifer is sitting down on a chair next to the kitchen table.

She is smoking a cigarette.

                    BRUCE (O.S.)
          Jennifer, I'm home.

Bruce enters the kitchen and finds her there. Jennifer puts out her cigarette and looks at him pitifully.

                    BRUCE
          What's wrong?

                    JENNIFER
          I just got a call from the hospital.
          They told me that my mother is dying.

BRUCE

Well, what the hell do you want me to do about it?

JENNIFER

Nothing. All I need is to be away for a few weeks to visit my mother before she passes.

BRUCE

You can't leave right now. I need you to stay here.

JENNIFER

Bruce, this is my mother... she's dying.

BRUCE

Listen, I just lost another deal with a major client... he fucked us over at the office by reneging on his payment. I'm not making the same kind of money that I used to and neither are you with the school teaching.

JENNIFER

Honey, it's not our fault that things are tough right now. The country is in a depression.

Bruce's voice rises.

BRUCE

You don't get it, damn it! The less money we have means less money to live on, less money for food, less money for rent. If I can't close a deal within the next month, even if I win a case, we are going to be kicked out on the street.

Jennifer tries to calm him down.

                    JENNIFER
I understand, but things will get better someday.

                    BRUCE
                    (Sighs)
I wish I could believe it, but I don't. We used to have
a beautiful little house out in Pasadena and making a
middle class income of a hundred fifty K a year. Now
we are stuck living in this Godforsaken shit hole and
can barely make it.

Bruce starts to get cynical.

                    BRUCE
Plus we're stuck in debt. I can't fucking take this anymore, I'd rather be dead.

Jennifer gets annoyed of Bruce's bad behavior.

                    JENNIFER
Don't say that! We've been through worse things than
this. I just lost my father and sister, now my doctor said
I can't even get pregnant.

                    BRUCE
What do you want?! Our lives are shit.

Bruce punches the wall with his fist, unable to handle the stress.

BRUCE

I called my father today -- the old rich bastard won't
even give us a loan. Penny-pinching prick.

He pulls out a plastic vial of cocaine from his inner coat pocket. He
pours it out on the table in front of Jennifer, not even caring that she's
his wife. He snorts a line of coke.

JENNIFER

What the hell? What are you doing?

BRUCE

Getting high. Got a problem with that?

Bruce snorts a second line of cocaine.

Jennifer gets upset and wipes the cocaine off the table.

BRUCE

What are you doing!

JENNIFER

You're using our money on drugs again!

BRUCE

Shut up, this relaxes me. You don't. You're not even
good in bed anymore!

JENNIFER

Stop it! Just stop it!

> BRUCE
>
> One of my clients couldn't pay me.
> So he gave me this instead. I didn't pay for it this time,
> okay?

Bruce pulls out five one hundred dollar bills and slams them on the table to prove his point.

> BRUCE
>
> Here, see? I told you I'm not lying.

Jennifer tries to reason with Bruce.

> JENNIFER
>
> I don't care if you got it for free or not. You're destroy-
> ing our marriage with this crap. Stop it Bruce, please
> -- I love you.

Bruce slaps her and slams her against the wall. He punches her in the face, giving her a black eye.

> BRUCE
>
> Stupid bitch! You're damn useless!
> You can't even give me a kid! Why the hell did I even
> marry you!

He storms off to the apartment and slams the door.

She breaks down emotionally. Jennifer lays hunched up on the floor, emotionally numbed by her husband's physical and verbal abuse.

> JENNIFER
>
> I'm sorry!

INT. BATHROOM - _DAY_

Jennifer washes her black eye in the sink. She is now wearing a pink shirt and bell bottom jeans. She looks at herself in the mirror. Wondering what to do about Bruce.

The phone rings in the kitchen.

Jennifer leaves the bathroom and heads to the kitchen.

INT. KITCHEN - CONTINUOUS

Jennifer goes to the phone and picks it up.

>   JENNIFER
>   Hello?

>   CARLA (V.O.)
>   Hey Jennifer.

>   JENNIFER
>   Carla.

>   CARLA (V.O.)
>   How you doing?

>   JENNIFER
>   Bruce just hit me.

>   CARLA (V.O.)
>   (Angrily)
>   Again?! That son-of-a-bitch!

JENNIFER

No, Carla. Its okay, he didn't mean it.

Carla sticks up with Jennifer and reasons with her.

CARLA (V.O.)

The hell he did not. Get yourself out of there, leave his worthless ass.

Jennifer gets defensive.

JENNIFER

I can't, he's just going through a lot of stress right now.

Carla scolds Jennifer about her abusive marriage.

CARLA (V.O.)

Oh yeah, you said that last month, and the month before that and the month before that. He's a ticking time bomb waiting to explode.

JENNIFER

That's not true.

CARLA (V.O.)

If you don't get out of there, you may come home one day and wake up with your throat slashed.

JENNIFER

What else can I do? I can't leave him. He needs me.

Carla mocks Jennifer.

CARLA (V.O.)

Bullshit! He's attorney, for God's sake. He doesn't deserve you. He should have an ungrateful wife who tries to ass rape him in court and suck him dry of his money.

JENNIFER

(screams)

Shut up! This is not what I called for. God, you can be a real bitch!

Jennifer calms down.

JENNIFER

I'm sorry. Look, I just got a call earlier that my mother is dying in the hospital.

CARLA (V.O.)

Holy shit. Do you need some help?

JENNIFER

Yes, I do.

CARLA (V.O.)

I could tell Stacy and Kelly. We could come down to see you.

JENNIFER

Thanks! I have to go out of town for a few days to visit my mom. Do you and the others want to come with me? We could get a hotel and maybe also try to take it easy for a week.

CARLA (V.O.)

Yeah sure. I'd be more than happy to go with you. I think the others would too.

JENNIFER

Thanks Carla. You're a good friend.

CARLA (V.O.)

Anytime. Get packed up, we'll meet you tomorrow afternoon in front of your place. Make sure that Bruce doesn't find out.

JENNIFER

I won't. I'll call the school and notify them of the issue. They'll have someone sub for me in the meantime.

CARLA (V.O.)

What about Bruce? Are you going to stay with him or leave him?

Jennifer pauses until she answers.

JENNIFER

I don't know.

CARLA (V.O.)

Wait, Jennifer?

Jennifer hangs up the phone.

INT. APARTMENT - _NIGHT_

The hours pass by on the clock until it's late at night with Jennifer waiting. Bruce does not come home.

Her phone rings, but she does not answer. The answering machine picks it up.

BEEP!

It's not Bruce. It's Carla!

                    CARLA (V.O.)
         Jennifer, it's Carla. Listen I talked to Stacy and Kelly
         and they will ride with us.

Carla speaks the truth about Bruce.

                    CARLA
         About Bruce, I don't trust him, I never did. One way or
         another he is going to leave you and cheat on you for
         another woman. You'll see.

Jennifer falls asleep on the couch in her small living room.

INT. APARTMENT - DAY

Jennifer wakes up. Bruce has still not come home.

INT. APARTMENT - LATER

Jennifer packs her suitcase in her bedroom and looks at the wall clock -- it shows 12 noon.

Jennifer leaves, until the phone rings.

RING!

The answering picks up the call. It's Bruce.

> BRUCE (V.O.)
> (sympathetic)
> Jennifer, it's Bruce. Listen, I'm sorry for what I did to
> you it wasn't right.

His voice starts to be demanding.

> BRUCE
> So please pick up the phone. If not, I should be on my
> way home as soon as possible and we'll talk, love you. Bye.

BEEP!

EXT. LOS ANGELES - DAY

A tricked out 1970 Chevrolet Chevelle classic car drives on an open highway exiting the city of Los Angeles and out to Moreno Valley.

EXT. INLAND EMPIRE - DAY

After hours of traffic, the Chevelle finally drives in the open highway.

INT. CHEVELLE - DAY

Jennifer is riding in the front passenger seat, while CARLA ESTRADA, 30, is driving. Two other girls, KELLY WINTERS, 24, and STACY TRAVIS, 27, are sitting in the back seat.

Carla, tough but sexy Latina and former MP who has been through hard times and got involved in more bar fights then any man has ever been.

Kelly, a fitness instructor and kick boxing tomboy. She inspires to be an MMA fighter.

Stacy, kind, animal loving, funny and charismatic neo-hippie.

She is the youngest and a college student from UCLA studying zoology.

Together, the girls are talking about each individual's situation, while traveling to Moreno Valley.

Kelly looks at Jennifer's bruises.

> KELLY
> I can't believe that Bruce hit you. If I were you, I'd kick his ass and wipe his face on the pavement.

Jennifer continues to defend Bruce.

> JENNIFER
> He wasn't always like this, you know.

> KELLY
> Why do you say that?

> JENNIFER
> When we first got together, he was real sweet.

> STACY
> (sarcastically)
> Please. A guy like that, he needs a therapist... not a human punching bag.

KELLY

If anyone should be a punching bag, it's him.

CARLA

We should all get together and beat the crap out of him. See how he likes it.

The girls laugh, all amused at the idea except Jennifer who repeatedly defends her husband.

JENNIFER

You guys are crazy; he'll have your asses thrown in jail so fast that you won't know what hit you.

KELLY

So what, Jen. It will be worth it.

Kelly laughs.

KELLY

(sarcastically)

I don't mind a bunch of prison dykes try to take me on.

(laughs)

Carla agrees with Kelly at first but she has second thoughts.

CARLA

Yeah, you're right. But it's still a fun idea.

All the girls start laughing.

JENNIFER

So what have you all been up to lately?

CARLA

I just lost my job at the base.

KELLY

That sucks.

CARLA

But I managed to get a temporary gig in the meantime.
I am dancing at this club downtown and doing some
modeling.

KELLY

How is the pay?

CARLA

The pay is decent, but the clientele are a bunch of
drunken assholes. But there is this one cute guy I like
at work.

JENNIFER

So what does he do?

CARLA

He is a bartender. His name is Miguel.

Jennifer turns her attention to Stacy.

JENNIFER

How about you, Stacy?

STACY

I've been teaching yoga out in Venice and painting. It's
fun but I wish I could meet a nice guy out there for once.

KELLY

What happen to Marty?

STACY

He fucked me, and then he dumped me, okay?

KELLY

Was he at least good?

STACY

No, not really. His dick was the size of an almond.

The girls laugh so hard it hurts.

STACY

He could barely put it in without cumming all over me.

CARLA

At least you're getting some. Jason left my ass and ran off with some nurse.

Jennifer turns her attention to Kelly.

JENNIFER

How 'bout you Kelly?

KELLY

Me, I've sworn off guys for a while.

So I'd rather try girls.

The girls are surprised of Kelly's coming out.

JENNIFER

Kelly?

CARLA

Damn. You're swinging now?

KELLY

Why bother staying with one guy when instead you can have the whole box of chocolate? Besides, girls kiss and fuck better, too. It's a fact, their sweet like chocolate and tasty as honey.

The girls are made awkward by Kelly's bisexuality.

Kelly didn't mind about her friends concern of her sexuality.

KELLY

Don't worry; you guys are not my type. Besides we've been friends since high school.

Carla turns her attention to Jennifer.

CARLA

I am so glad that we were able to find some time to hang out.

JENNIFER
(Sad)

Yeah...

STACY

Oh come on you guys. Enough of this depressing chit chat. Let's have some fun. Hey Carla, hit the radio.

Carla turns on the radio and classic rock station.

EXT. INLAND EMPIRE - DAY

The Chevelle drives up to a traffic signal in San Bernardino.

A 1972 El Camino Low Rider, with a pair of young styling GANG BANGERS drives on the other side of the street. One of the gang bangers taunts Carla, by banging on the side of his door.

> GANG BANGER #1
> Hey pussycat. Do you wanna come fly with me?

> CARLA
> Dream on, puto.

The gang banger continues to taunt her.

> GANG BANGER #1
> Aw come on Lolita! Let's race; you got a sweet ride over
> there. How 'bout this, if you win we leave you alone.
> But if we win, you and your chicas come fly with us.

The girls except Jennifer smile at the gang bangers. One of the gang bangers notices Jennifer looking back.

> GANG BANGER #2
> How 'bout your friend in the front seat? Maybe she can
> use a little company.

Carla responds to the gang banger's challenge.

CARLA

Deal. Let's ride.

JENNIFER

What are you doing?

CARLA

Relax, we'll smoke 'em.

The Chevelle and the El Camino rev up their engine waiting for the light to turn green.

The light turns green. Both cars race.

The El Camino is ahead while the Chevelle is trailing.

Carla shifts gears and makes several turns. The girls are having fun, including Jennifer.

The Chevelle finally gets ahead of the El Camino and wins.

The girls celebrate their victory as they drive off to Moreno Valley into the sunset.

The gang bangers are disappointed.

GANG BANGER #1

Damn!

GANG BANGER #2

Got smoked by a bunch of chicas.

DOMINIC R. DANIELS & RON DELEON

INT. CHEVELLE - DAY

The girls celebrate their victory. Kelly and Stacy give hi fives.

                    CARLA
        I told you, I'd smoked em and you didn't believe me.

Jennifer is finally having the time of her life, enjoy with friends.

                    STACY
        So how long is Moreno Valley?

                    CARLA
        About two hours depending on traffic and timing?

Unfortunately, there is a traffic jam. A major accident has blocked the
freeway. Cars are not moving.

                    CARLA
        Shit!

                    JENNIFER
        How long it's going to take?

                    CARLA
        How the fuck do I know? We're stuck. I hope it doesn't
        take long.

                    KELLY
        Wake me up when we get to Moreno Valley.

Kelly takes a nap. The girls have to wait for the traffic to clear.

EXT. FREEWAY - DAY

The traffic stops between Los Angeles and the Inland Empire it could take hours to clear.

EXT. HIGHWAY - NIGHT

It is 8pm at night. The girls are tired but they are almost to their destination. Until the Chevelle breaks down and engine goes out.

Carla struggles to stop the car while the other girls wake up totally spooked.

                         KELLY
          What the hell?!

                         CARLA
          I can't stop it.

Carla pushes the brakes hard and pulls the hand brake -- the tires screech hard with smoke emitting underneath from them.

The girls scream.

Finally the car stops on the side of the road in the middle of nowhere. The girls have a road map and no cell phone.

INT. CHEVELLE - NIGHT

The girls breathe heavily, relieved but not killed.

                         CARLA
          Is everyone alright?

JENNIFER
Yeah I think so.

Kelly get upset at Carla.

KELLY
Why the hell did you do that Carla?!

CARLA
The transmission must have burned out.

KELLY
Shit, thanks a lot Carla.

STACY
If you didn't race those guys back there, we wouldn't
be stuck here.

CARLA
Hey quit you're moping, thank God we didn't get killed.

Jennifer pulls out her cell phone but it's dead. She forgot the charger at
home.

JENNIFER
So what do we do now? Anyone got a cell phone? Mine
is dead.

The girls pull out there pockets.

ALL THE GIRLS
(in unison)
No.

KELLY

I left mine at home.

CARLA

I can't afford one.

STACY

I don't even own one.

Jennifer is frustrated.

JENNIFER

Then how are we going to get help?

CARLA

Relax; I got a road map and a flashlight, with some flares in the trunk.

Carla gets out of the car.

EXT. HIGHWAY - NIGHT

The Chevelle headlights are still on. Carla goes to the back of the car and opens the trunk. She grabs the flashlight, a road map and a couple of road flares. She goes to the front of the car. She turns on the flashlight and places the map on the hood.

The other girls get out of the car to assist Carla.

Carla points her flashlight on the map.

CARLA

We should be right here.

Carla points her finger at the center of the map, between Moreno Valley and Riverside.

KELLY
(sarcastic)
Great, we are in the middle of nowhere, out in the country.

JENNIFER
Now where are we going to get help?

Carla looks at the map.

CARLA
There is a gas station with an auto shop less than a mile from here.

JENNIFER
What about the car?

CARLA
We'll push it behind those bushes over there so no one steals it.

Carla goes to the driver's seat and shifts it to neutral.

CARLA
You guys. Help me push it into the bushes and we'll start walking.

The girls push the car to the back of the bushes, while Carla steers the car.

After the car stops, Carla gets out with the keys and locks the door.

The girls start walking down on the side of the empty pitch black highway in the moonlight, with their flashlight.

EXT. AUTO SHOP - NIGHT

Ten minutes later they make it down to an old and dimly lit rundown gas station and auto garage that has seen way better days. There is a light on in the main office window with the sound of classic rock playing inside.

STACY
Look, there's a light on. Let's check it out.

The girls go to the front porch, knock on the screen door and ring the buzzer.

The screen door opens and to their surprise there stands a young and handsome MECHANIC, mid 30s, dressed in a mechanic jump suit. He has the slick charm and coolness of James Dean.

MECHANIC
Good evening ladies. Is there something I can help you with?

The girls are stunned by the mechanic's good looks. Carla speaks.

CARLA
Our car just broke down. Can you help us fix it?

MECHANIC
Sure, I'll be glad to. For the right money. I'm technically closed, it's eight o' clock.

                    JENNIFER
        Aw come on, please?

Jennifer pulls out $200.

                    JENNIFER
        This is all we got... can you help us please?

The Mechanic thinks about it.

                    MECHANIC
        For two hundred dollars, I'll fix your car and even put
        ribbons on it.

Jennifer hands the cash to the mechanic.

                    MECHANIC
        Where's your car at?

                    CARLA
        Outside in the bushes, on the road heading towards
        your place.

                    MECHANIC
        Okay, we'll take my tow truck and haul it down here. I
        need one of you to show me where the car is.

                    JENNIFER
        I'll go.

                    MECHANIC
        The rest of you can wait here inside the office. By the
        way, I'm Russell.

JENNIFER

I'm Jennifer. This is Carla, Stacy and Kelly.

RUSSELL (MECHANIC)

My pleasure.

STACY

Finally -- it's nice to meet a gentleman for once.

Jennifer goes with Russell, while the rest of the girls watch them go.

CARLA

Whoa, this guy is hot!

KELLY

Tell me about it.

STACY

I thought you like girls, Kelly.

KELLY

I do, but right now if I was given choice, I'd love to fuck him.

Russell overhears the girls' conversation.

RUSSELL

I'll take that as a compliment.

The girls blush a little. Russell and Jennifer get into the tow truck and drive to the highway.

STACY

So what does Russell do during his spare time besides fixing cars?

KELLY

I don't know but we'll sure find out. Is he married?

CARLA

Who cares? As long as he's good looking and yummy.

STACY

Too bad, Jennifer is with him right now. Probably flirting with him.

CARLA

Doubtful.

INT. TOW TRUCK - NIGHT

Russell is driving while Jennifer is in the passenger's seat navigating.

RUSSELL

So, where are you and your girlfriends from?

JENNIFER

L.A.

RUSSELL

What brings you out to the middle of nowhere?

JENNIFER

My mom lives in Moreno Valley. We're going out to visit her a while and also try to kick back for a few days.

RUSSELL

Well, you're not going to find too much to do out here
in the Inland Empire, except get drunk and laid.
Not too much to do for entertainment.

JENNIFER

I'll think I'll pass on that.

EXT. HIGHWAY - NIGHT

The tow truck drives on the middle of the highway, where the bushes
are, and drives around to the Chevelle.

Russell gets out of the truck and hooks the car on the front chrome
bumper, while Jennifer waits in the truck. Russell gets back in and
drives off, towing the Chevelle back to the auto shop.

EXT. AUTO SHOP - NIGHT

BOOMER, a hunting dog and bloodhound, arrives in the front porch
chained up.

Stacy comes out of the auto shop and pets the dog.

STACY

Hey big boy.

Boomer sniffs her and immediately growls. He bites her hand instantly.

STACY

Oww!

Stacy stands back, while Kelly arrives, witnessing the attack, and about
to assault the dog for what it did to Stacy.

Russell and Jennifer come back to the chop shop while the girls walk out of the office. Russell and Jennifer get out of the truck.

RUSSELL

Damn it Boomer you dumb mutt.

Russell spanks the dog on the back, causing the dog to yelp.

RUSSELL

Bad dog!

Stacy flips out while holding the wound.

STACY

Hey what are you doing? He doesn't know any better!

RUSSELL

Sorry about that... Boomer doesn't like strangers. Especially women.

Russell goes inside the tow truck and pulls out a small glass flask of whiskey and a clean rag from his glove compartment.

RUSSELL

Here, take this. That will kill the bacteria before it gets infected.

STACY

Thanks.

Stacy takes the bottle and pours it on her wound, then she cleans it with a rag. Stacy winces a little in pain. Carla arrives from the office.

CARLA

So what is wrong with the car?

RUSSELL

Let me take a look.

Russell unhitches the Chevelle and looks underneath the hood.

JENNIFER

We think it's the transmission that is shot.

RUSSELL

Yep, you're right about that.

CARLA

How long is it going to take to fix?

RUSSELL

Probably a day or two. The only problem is the parts; I
don't have them available for this type of car.
I'll have to order them.

The girls get frustrated as they have nowhere else to go.

CARLA

Where can we find the nearest motel?

RUSSELL

About twenty miles from here.

The girls are tired and worried.

CARLA

Can we call a cab?

RUSSELL

You could if the phone was working. Don't you ladies have cell phones?

JENNIFER

Mine died; I left my charger at home.

RUSSELL

How bout you?

CARLA

We don't have any cell phones, I can't afford them. Do you?

RUSSELL

Nope. Never have, never will.

CARLA

(upset)

Great! Where are we going to stay for the night?

Russell offers them shelter inside the auto shop.

RUSSELL

You ladies can stay here for the night. Sleep in the office and I'll camp out in my tow truck. It's not the most comfortable of accommodations but it's better than being stuck out freezing in the cold.

Kelly wraps her arms.

KELLY

He's right you know. It's getting cold.

The rest of the girls agree with him.

CARLA

Okay, we'll stay for the night. We'll try to work something out tomorrow.

JENNIFER

Thank you for your hospitality.

RUSSELL

There is one thing that my father taught me. Always respect a lady.

The girls go inside the auto shop, while Russell goes to his tow truck to sleep.

RUSSELL

(to himself)

Lovely ladies, aren't they. Lovely.

INT. OFFICE - NIGHT

The girls enter the office. Inside it has a couch, a small bed, a desk, a lamp, a phone, a radio and a chair. Jennifer sleeps on the couch, while Carla and Stacy share the bed and Kelly sleeps on the chair.

She checks the phone -- it's dead.

CARLA

In the morning, we'll ask Russell if he can drop us off at the motel.

STACY

He won't be able to take us all at once.

CARLA

Then we'll have to walk then.

KELLY

Hey girls... do you want to get to know Russell a little bit better?

STACY

I don't, after what he did to that dog.

KELLY

Hey, he bit you. That stupid dog deserved it! You're such a damn hippie.

STACY

Dyke.

Kelly is about to hit Stacy.

CARLA

Come on you two. Cut it out.

Carla breaks up the argument. Kelly sits down.

KELLY

Okay, since you don't want to get to know Russell, Stacy, then all three of us will. Especially Jennifer, since Bruce won't give any to her.

Jennifer flips the bird at her friends.

Kelly and Stacy begin to toy with Jennifer.

KELLY

Just fucking with you, Jen. We know you're married. Damn.

Kelly attempts to lighten up Jennifer.

KELLY

But seriously, get rid of Bruce for once. This is time for ourselves.

STACY

Yeah, Bruce is probably banging a girl right now in some hotel. That's what I predict.

KELLY

By the way, Jen -- did you make a move with Russell back there?

Jennifer gets annoyed at Kelly's teasing.

JENNIFER
(yelling)
Why don't you all grow up?!

Stacy and Kelly paused. Jennifer gets defensive.

JENNIFER

Look I love my husband, despite his problems, or what's wrong with him. None of you have been married before. You don't understand.

Carla backs up Jennifer.

CARLA

She's right.

KELLY

(sympathetic)

Sorry.

JENNIFER

(calms down)

It's okay. Hey. Let's try to get some sleep and worry about this tomorrow, okay. Good night.

KELLY

Okay, okay. Good night.

The girls go to sleep. Kelly turns off the lamp light.

INT. AUTO SHOP - NIGHT

The auto shop lights go off. The area is PITCH BLACK caused by a power outage. An UNKNOWN FIGURE shuts down the power at an electric box. He is armed with a hunting rifle with a sniper scope.

Kelly wakes up and hears a noise from outside. She goes outside with Carla's flashlight, while the rest of the girls sleep.

EXT. AUTO SHOP - NIGHT

Kelly comes outside with the flashlight on to survey the scene. She sees the tow truck.

> KELLY
> (whispers)
> Russell... are you there?

No response. Russell is not in his tow truck but she finds blood inside. Kelly checks the garage but the door is locked.

She knocks on the door.

> KELLY
> Russell!

Again no response. Kelly finds blood below the garage door.

Something is not right. Then, she finds footprints on the ground and follows them in the dark -- they lead into the darkness.

She finds the electric box turned off. She tries to turns it back on. The lights flick dimly and go back out. To her great surprise, she finds the phone line cut.

> KELLY
> What the hell?

Right that moment, a hunting knife pierces through Kelly's back. Blood comes out through her mouth -- she chokes on her own blood.

Kelly crawls to the ground struggling to get help. She tries to crawl back to the auto shop but she can't move an inch.

She is paralyzed.

The UNKNOWN FIGURE arrives, but we don't see his face. He slowly and silently walks to Kelly with a big sledge hammer.

He raises it up slowly and...

SPLAT!

The UNKNOWN FIGURE smashes Kelly's skull into chunks of blood,_ _flesh, bone and brains. Drenching the grass in crimson-stained gore.

INT. OFFICE - NIGHT

The girls wake up as they hear a noise.

> JENNIFER
>
> Did you hear that?

> CARLA
>
> Hear what?

> JENNIFER
>
> Something is outside.

CARLA

Maybe it's just that dog barking. No big deal. Don't worry.

The girls realize that Kelly is missing.

JENNIFER

Where's Kelly?

CARLA

I don't know, turn the light on.

Jennifer goes to the lamp and tries to turn it back on.

JENNIFER

That's strange, the power is out.

STACY

You guys, I can't see anything. What's going on?

CARLA

I don't have my flashlight, Kelly must have took it. Let's go outside and check it out.

The trio heads outside.

EXT. AUTO SHOP - NIGHT

The girls come outside. It's pitch black with only moonlight to guide them.

JENNIFER

Kelly?!

STACY

She probably went to take a piss.

CARLA

That's an awful long piss.

JENNIFER

Something is not right... she's been gone for an hour.

CARLA

Let's check the restroom.

The girls check the other side of the building where it has a restroom. They knock on the door but it is unlocked.

They open the door and see nothing but a foul-smelling restroom. They are disgusted.

STACY

Ewww, gross!

CARLA

No she's not there.

STACY

Russell may be a good-looking guy but he sure needs to know how to clean. Yuck.

Carla shuts down the door. The trio goes back to the front porch.

CARLA

She has to be playing hide and seek. Kelly?! Where are you?! This isn't a game. Stop fooling around!

JENNIFER

Look.

Jennifer looks at the electric box, and leads the girls to that destination. Then, suddenly she steps into something squishy.

JENNIFER

What did I just step in?

STACY

I don't know.. Dog shit?

Carla finds her flashlight.

CARLA

There is my flashlight.

Carla turns on her flashlight and they all see the decapitated body of Kelly.

All the girls scream in terror and run like crazy.

The girls run to the tow truck to find Russell. Jennifer bangs on the window.

STACY
(panicking)
Oh my God! Oh my God!

JENNIFER

Russell! Help!

No response. Russell is not there.

Jennifer sees the blood in the tow truck.

The UNKNOWN FIGURE pulls out his sniper hunting rifle and points it at the girls.

BANG!

Glass shatters -- A shot hits one of the headlights on the tow truck, spooking the girls out.

The UNKNOWN FIGURE begins to hear voices in his head relive his past as a living nightmare. He hears voices of military orders, people screaming, and war in Iraq and Afghanistan.

He goes ballistic and is ready for the hunt, but first he drags the body of Kelly away from the area.

INT. AUTO SHOP - NIGHT

Jennifer, Carla and Stacey enter the auto shop and locks it up.

CARLA

Where is he?!

STACY

I don't know, they must have got him too.

JENNIFER

She's right, didn't you see the blood on his windshield.

CARLA

Come on guys, find some weapons.

They scramble to find any weapons to defend themselves but there are none.

                    CARLA
        Shit, there is nothing to defend ourselves.

The Unknown Figure shadow in behind the window.

The girls duck and cover. Stacy hides behind the door.

                    STACY
                  (panicking)
            What do we do! What do we do!

                    CARLA
    Shh!

KNOCK!

THUD!

The Unknown Figure tries to open the door. Somehow...He unlocks it.

He smashes the window and grabs Stacy.

Stacy screams but escapes.

The girls scream. -- They go to the back door and escape.

EXT. LARGE WEED FIELD - NIGHT

Jennifer, Carla and Stacey continue to run in the middle of nowhere. They are in a large weed field. Carla is leading the team with only her flashlight. They are all scared.

                              STACY
                           (panicking)
What the fuck was that?!

                              CARLA
I don't know, but whoever got Kelly and Russell is coming after us.

                             JENNIFER
Let's just go to the motel and be safe there.

                              CARLA
I left my map in the car... the motel is probably 20 to 30 miles from here, who knows where we are.

                              STACY
Damn.

                             JENNIFER
Do you know where we're going?

                              CARLA
I don't know, but if we don't stop moving, that psychopath is going to pick us off one by one. Let's go.

Carla looks at the moon.

                              CARLA
Follow the moonlight.

Carla leads Jennifer and Stacy to travel east in the middle of the Inland Empire by foot.

EXT. LARGE FOREST - NIGHT

The gray moon brightens. After about an hour of travel, the girls have reached to a large forest.

Carla and Jennifer are calm but scared. Stacy is freaking out. Together they are all trying to figure out who is stalking them.

                         CARLA
          That Russell guy. What a waste...

                         JENNIFER
          ...and Kelly. Who do you think killed them?

                         CARLA
          I don't know. Looks like we got a serial killer we're
          dealing with.

                         STACY
          Oh my God!

                         CARLA
          Chill Stacy.

                         JENNIFER
          What about those gang bangers back in San Bernardino?
          Do you think they did it?

                         CARLA
          No I don't think so.

                         JENNIFER
          They probably did. You pissed them off when you
          raced them.

CARLA

Hey, they started it. Beside, that was no pistol or Colt 45 that we were shot at with. It sounded more like a hunting rifle.

JENNIFER

How can you tell?

Carla talks about her military experience.

CARLA

Back in Afghanistan... our base was attacked by Taliban soldiers who were hiding in the mountains. There were snipers everywhere and we could see them. We sent air support to wipe out the mountains.

Stacy gets tired. Her feet are getting numb. Jennifer looks back.

JENNIFER

Stacy.

Jennifer goes to Stacy and picks her up, while Carla is still walking.

JENNIFER

Come on, Stacy. We got to keep moving.

STACY

I can't go on any further.

JENNIFER

Let's go find some water.

The girls travel to an isolated lake. They drink the water despite of it being dirty and ice cold.

Carla is guessing who is stalking them.

CARLA

I think I know who is doing this.
Have you heard of The Butcher of Los Angeles?

JENNIFER

No. Who is he?

CARLA

A year ago, he was a hunter who killed for sport. He massacred people at an unemployment office. No one's seen him ever since.

JENNIFER

And then what happened?

CARLA

The Butcher starts killing victims with no trace of the bodies.

JENNIFER

How do you know all this?

CARLA

I heard in on the news. A few weeks ago, a tow truck driver was found dead in the middle of the night some-where in the Inland Empire. All they found was his head upper torso.

JENNIFER

So he could be here.

Stacy gets frightened as she shivers.

CARLA
Wait right here, I'll scout the area.

Carla leaves the team as she survey the scene.

Then, they hear a dog barking.

STACY
Did you hear that?

JENNIFER
Yeah.

The dog arrives and sees the girls. It's Boomer.

STACY
It's Boomer! Boomer, come here fella.

JENNIFER
Didn't that dog bite you?

STACY
I'm sure he didn't mean it.
(to Boomer)
Come here boy.

Stacy walks towards Boomer to give him a hug. But... Boomer attacks her and bites off her shirt and goes rabid, foaming at the mouth.

STACY
Ahh! Help! Jennifer help!

Jennifer doesn't respond as she just stands there and watches paralyzed with fear.

STACY
(to Jennifer)
Don't just stand there and help me!

Carla notices that Stacy is in trouble -- she rushes in and saves Stacy. Carla pulls Boomer away from Stacy as she wrestles with the dog. Finally, she hits Boomer. He yelps and runs away.

Carla catches a deep breath as she helps Stacy get up, with minor scratches and bruises.

CARLA

Are you okay?

STACY

(crying)
I'm fine. I'm never trusting dogs again.

CARLA
I thought you love all animals.

STACY

Yes, but not this one.

Carla and Stacy looks at Jennifer in disappointment. Carla confronts Jennifer while she is still standing.

CARLA

Why did you not help Stacy when she was attacked, huh? What were you thinking? You just stood there doing nothing.

Stacy comes to Jennifer's defense.

STACY

Carla, leave her alone, she was scared.

CARLA

To hell with that, you almost got killed. Thanks to your animal-loving, hippie bullshit. We just lost Kelly -who's going to be next?

STACY

Carla, you are starting to act like Jennifer's asshole of a husband.

Jennifer snaps as she yells out loud.

JENNIFER

You guys, stop it! I'm sorry for not helping you! Let's just get out of here!

BANG!

A rifle gunshot hits a tree, just missing the girls. The girls scream in terror as they resume running away.

The unknown figure reloads his rifle as he continues to hunt for the girls.

The girls continue to run with no time to argue.

BANG! BANG! BANG!

The unknown figure continues to fire at the girls but misses.

The girls are terrified as the adrenaline rush kicks in.

EXT. INLAND EMPIRE - NIGHT

It is late at night. The girls leave the forest and head to a grassy field. They are tired as hell and they still can't find a place to hide.

STACY

We've been walking for hours. Where are we?

CARLA

I don't know.

JENNIFER

Hey you guys, there is a junkyard.

They find an old abandoned junk yard near a grass and dirt area. Piles of old smashed up cars scattered.

There are cars where they can hide from their unknown hunter.

JENNIFER

Looks abandoned.

CARLA

Abandoned or not, let take our chances. We don't have a choice, we got to find a phone to call the police.

STACY

I don't like this.

CARLA

Do you all want to stay here and get shot?!

ALL THE GIRLS

No!

                              CARLA
        Let's move then.

The girls open the gate and enter the junkyard. Little do they know, a sign is posted: "Beware: No Trespassing Allowed".

EXT. JUNKYARD - NIGHT

The trio searches for a place to hide for the night.

                              CARLA
        Split up, we need to find at least a decent enough ve-
        hicle to hide in until daylight.

Jennifer, Carla and Stacy split up to find a place to hide.

Unknown to them, there are hidden booby traps and land mines that are surrounding the area.

Carla continues her search.

Stacy is able to find a small RV trailer, but it's not in working condition.

                              STACY
        Hey you guys! I found something!

It's a trailer!

Carla and Jennifer reunite with Stacy.

EXT. INLAND EMPIRE - NIGHT

The unknown figure hears Stacy's yelling. He follows the noise which leads him to the junkyard.

EXT. JUNKYARD - NIGHT

Carla and Jennifer rendezvous with Stacy in the trailer.

CARLA
Good work. Let's look for a phone inside.

STACY
This old RV doesn't even look like it works.

CARLA
Well we gotta to try anyway. If we don't, we're dead.
Now come on.

All three girls open the RV trailer door and enter. They lock the trailer shut.

INT. OLD RV TRAILER - NIGHT

The girls are looking for anything they can use as weapons to defend themselves, as well as a phone to call the police with in the cramped RV trailer, but they find nothing.

Carla's flashlight dies down. She hits the flashlight to try to get power back but it's no good.

Stacy finds a first aid kit. She heals her wounds.

CARLA
Great, the light's gone out.

Jennifer, use your cell phone.

JENNIFER
It's dead you idiot!

                    CARLA
    Oh yeah, I forgot. Let's see if it's still piece of junk is
    still working.

Jennifer goes to the front of the RV trailer alone. She tries to find the
keys of the RV but nothing. Then she tries to hot wire the RV, again it
doesn't work.

                    CARLA
    I guess we have to sleep here 'til dawn.

The RV is out of commission. Jennifer bangs her head on the steering
wheel.

                    CARLA
    What's her problem?

                    STACY
    I guess the fight we had earlier pissed her off.

Carla goes to Jennifer, while Stacy goes to the bunk bed.

She attempts to reason with Jennifer about the dog attack incident.

                    CARLA
    Jennifer, look I am sorry for yelling and being hard at
    you. I am upset that we lost a friend and I didn't want
    to lose another.

Jennifer doesn't look at Carla as she sulks and gives Carla the cold shoulder. She takes this personally.

CARLA

Listen, we'll make it out of this together and see your mother... okay?

Carla tries to hug Jennifer but she refuses. Carla gets insulted by Jennifer's sulking.

CARLA

I know that you're mad at me, but you got to realize that you can't let yourself be stepped on for the rest of your life. Stand up for yourself. You think you've had it hard, look at me.

Carla tells her story to make amends.

CARLA

I lost my job, I lost custody of my kid, my boyfriend left me, my parents don't want to talk to me. I have nothing left to lose. Until, the day you step up and take control of your life, you are going to remain nothing but a victim.

Jennifer doesn't respond to Carla's advice.

Carla leaves Jennifer in frustration.

CARLA

I give up.

Carla slips in the other half of the bunk bed. Stacy finished healing her wounds.

STACY

So how'd it go?

CARLA

Jennifer is still shaken up. When is she going to get some guts?

STACY

You should leave her alone...

CARLA

Hey, if it wasn't for me, you would have been mauled by that dog. I did what I had to do.

STACY

(insulting)

You can be a real bitch sometimes.
You know that.

CARLA

Forget it. Look, let's just get some sleep 'til morning. Maybe he'll give up and go away.

STACY

(frighten)

I'm scared.

CARLA

Don't worry; we'll make it out alive.

Carla and Stacy sleep while Jennifer is wide awake thinking.

EXT. INLAND EMPIRE - NIGHT

SERIES OF SHOTS

The UNKNOWN FIGURE assembles his hunting rifle.

Puts on his mask and hunting gear.

Loads his rifle with bullets.

The Unknown Figure is ready to kill...

EXT. JUNKYARD - NIGHT

The Unknown Figure enters the junkyard to search and destroy the girls. He is still armed with his hunting rifle. At the same time, he remembers his days in Iraq. He has another hallucination.

FLASHBACK - EXT. IRAQI BATTLEFIELD - DAY

UNKNOWN FIGURE POV

The unknown figure is serving in Iraq. We still don't see his face, just his hands and guns. He is hunting for insurgent rebels.

He shoots a lot of Iraqis, men, women and children alike. He goes insane. He enjoys the screams and pain of innocent Iraqis.

IRAQI WOMAN
Please!!! Don't kill us!!!

He shoots the Iraqi Woman in the head, as her brains are splattered.

He see wounded U.S. Soldiers.

The screen fades out.

EXT. JUNKYARD - NIGHT (BACK TO PRESENT)

The unknown figure stops having his hallucination. He continues to hunt the girls, searches each car one by one.

INT. OLD RV TRAILER - NIGHT

Jennifer who is still awake looks at the window and sees the unknown figure and his face. She is shocked at what she has seen. She quietly warns the girls.

> JENNIFER
> (whispers)
> Carla... Stacy...

Carla is still tired.

> CARLA
> (grumbles)
> Not now...

> JENNIFER
> (whispers)
> You're not going to believe this... the killer is... is...

> CARLA
> Is here?

Jennifer nods her head.

CRASH!

The unknown figure shoots the side window. He shoots again but runs out of bullets.

The girls wake up and scream in terror.

The Unknown Figure firmly holds the hunting rifle and continues to shoot the RV Trailer.

STACY
(screaming)
Run!!!!

They go out the back door of the RV.

Jennifer is the last to leave, but the unknown figure grabs grabs her. The two wrestled. The unknown figure pins her down.

Jennifer takes off his mask revealing and his face... It's Russell Maddox. She is shocked at what she has seen.

Russell smiles.

RUSSELL
Surprised?

Jennifer knees him in the groin -- She escapes.

Carla and Stacy hide in one of the cars. They notice Jennifer is missing.

CARLA
Where's Jennifer?

Jennifer pops up, reuniting with the other girls.

                    JENNIFER
                  (whispering)
I know who it is.

                     CARLA
                  (whispering)
Who is it?

                    JENNIFER
                  (whispering)
It's Russell.

                     CARLA
                  (whispering)
Are you serious?

                    JENNIFER
                  (whispering)
I'm dead serious.

EXT. JUNKYARD - NIGHT

Russell gets up, recovering from the groin hit. -- He scouts around the area to find the girls.

Carla and Stacy see him for themselves.

                     STACY
                  (whispering)
Oh shit, Jennifer is right.

                     CARLA
                  (whispering)
Quiet.

Together, they team up to find a way to outwit and kill Russell.

CARLA
(whispering)
The moment he loses us we get out of the junkyard and keep running until we get help.

Russell is reloading his rifle.

Then, Boomer smells Stacys blood and spot the girls location.

Boomer barks, and Jennifer, Carla and Stacy run away.

CARLA
Run!

Russell sees them.

RUSSELL
It's play time, girls!

Russell chases the girls.

Jennifer and Carla manage to escape, with Stacy running behind them.

STACY
Guys wait!

Stacy stumbles through a pile of trash on the ground and falls into a covered dug out pit in the ground. Instantly killed -- landing on a spiked pit trap from sawed off sharp metal pipes impaling her right through her chest, legs and neck as blood sprays everywhere. She dies.

The remaining girls split up with Russell trying to shoot them with his rifle. But he finds out his bullets have run out.

RUSSELL
That's right whores. Run away...
I'm coming for ya.

He laughs sickly and chases after them with his hunting knife while Boomer continues to chase after the girls.

Meanwhile Jennifer manages to find an old abandoned junk car to hide in. While trying to remain still, she thinks that they are safe but...

BOOM!

Russell smashes the side window with a monkey wrench.

Jennifer screams in terror and they go out the right passenger side of the car and manage to escape.

Meanwhile, Carla runs to the tow truck, which has no keys.

She attempts to hotwire the car but does not have time.

Russell slowly walks towards Carla.

Carla finds a crowbar in the passenger side and grabs it.

She gets out of the truck and attacks Russell. She knocks the knife out of his hand and she hits him in the back, knocking him to the ground. She attempts to smash his skull open but he dodges the attack and punches her in the face causing her to lose her crowbar.

CARLA

You motherfucker! I'll fucking kill you!

RUSSELL

Come on bitch! Time to die.

Carla and Russell go hand to hand combat. Russell gains the upper hand and kicks her in the stomach. Carla grabs Russell's knife and stabs him in the lower thigh and runs off. Russell screams in pain.

She takes off and stumbles causing her to drop the knife but is able to pick up her crowbar. She hears Jennifer screaming for help.

JENNIFER

Carla!

While running, Jennifer runs close by two buried land mines that go off and she manage to dodge the explosions with sheer dumb luck, now terrified beyond belief.

Boomer runs across a buried land mine that he activates and it blows him to pieces.

BOOM!

Jennifer runs back into the auto shop.

Wounded, Russell searches the junkyard only to find Boomers bloody and gory remains.

RUSSELL

(mourning)

Boomer...damn bitches...

Then, he hears another voice over in his head reliving his past as a soldier in Iraq.

                    RUSSELL
          I'm at K-9 Romero, my squad just got taken out by insurgent rebels. I got civilians dying on me. Send help, over!

Russell hears voices of war in his head -- switches in his mind, hearing the screams of women and children as they are slaughtered. He hears the echoes of the dead wailing in his mind.

FLASHBACK - EXT. IRAQI BATTLEFIELD - DAY

Russell, in his military fatigues, is the last man standing in a bloody standoff between Taliban rebels and the US military. His squad fires a rocket attack in an open area where the enemy is killing many opposing soldiers blowing them to pieces.

                    RUSSELL
          I repeat, send reinforcements!

Suddenly, the smoke clears -- Russell and his team run to survey the area.

                    RUSSELL
                 (to his men)
          Check the area.

Then out of nowhere from all different sides more Taliban pop up and fire their AK-47's cutting the US soldiers to pieces with blood and guts flying everywhere.

Then one of the enemy soldiers comes from behind Russell and knocks him out with the butt of his rifle. He is captured by Taliban.

Russell forced to the ground on his knees with his hands

tied behind his back. He is forced to see one of his soldiers, a friend, butchered right in front of him, while struggling.

SERIES OF SHOTS

Three Taliban soldiers arrive and restrain the captured soldier and de-capitate him slowly...

They slit his throat like a chicken...

The blood sprays out all over the place including Russell...

Russell screams in terror...

Finally, the Taliban cuts the guy's head and Russell is traumatized be-yond belief...

The Taliban remove their masks and much to Russell's surprise, they are women! Beautiful women in their twenties. The female Taliban take Russell to a holding cell.

Russell imagines Jennifer and Carla are the female Taliban.

EXT. JUNKYARD - NIGHT (BACK TO PRESENT)

Russell returns to reality, enraged at the girls, after seeing his prize dog killed -- he goes ballistic, raving like a lunatic to slaughter the girls alive and torture them to death.

RUSSELL

Boomer!!! No!!! You cunts killed my dog!!!

He searches the entire area.

RUSSELL

When I find you both, I'm going to rip you limb from limb and shred you to pieces!!!

He reloads his weapons and is ready to kill.

EXT. JUNKYARD OFFICE - NIGHT

Jennifer is exhausted and unable to travel to the auto shop.

Jennifer finds the lit caretaker's office and enters.

INT. JUNKYARD OFFICE - NIGHT

The office is a rundown 1980s office with dust and cobwebs.

Jennifer tries to call the police on the land line phone but the operator on the line is nothing but an automated message.

OPERATOR (V.O.)

The phone connection you are using is no longer in service. If you need help please try again and dial for the operator.

Jennifer hangs up the phone.

JENNIFER

Come on! Damn it! You got to be kidding!

The phone is out of service. Then, a stranger enters the junk yard office. Jennifer hides underneath the table.

The stranger opens the door and enters the room and calls out her name.

UNKNOWN WOMAN (O.S.)
Jennifer.

It is a woman's voice. Jennifer recognizes it's Carla. The two reunite.

JENNIFER
Carla!

CARLA
Jennifer!

The two friends hug each other out of relief.

JENNIFER
Thank God you're alright!

CARLA
Where's Stacy?

JENNIFER
We got to find her and get out of here. But let's stick together.

The girls run around the area close to each other calling out to find Stacy.

EXT. JUNKYARD - NIGHT

Carla and Jennifer search for Stacy in the junkyard.

CARLA

Stacy!!!

JENNIFER

Stacy!!!

CARLA

Where are you!!!

No luck. Until they run to the open pit that Stacy fell in.

Jennifer sees her mutilated body and cringes with fear.

JENNIFER

Jesus!

CARLA

What is it?

Carla sees Stacy and is enraged. Jennifer buries her face in her arm.

CARLA

Damn bastard, he killed her. He's toying with us.

JENNIFER

No... he's hunting us.

BANG! SPLAT!

Suddenly Russell shows up and begins to fire at the girls!

Carla gets hit in the leg and falls to the ground in pain, wounded and bleeding. Carla screams in pain.

JENNIFER

Carla!!!

Russell is about to fire another shot but he's run out of bullets -- he goes back to his truck to reload.

JENNIFER

Carla, stay with me.

CARLA

Go! Leave me!

JENNIFER

No, I won't leave you.

CARLA

Just fucking run!

Jennifer begins to toughen up, assuming leadership over the two... finally able to stand up for herself, and she's tired of being a victim.

JENNIFER

Back to the office. Come on! Lean on me!

Carla puts her shoulder around Jennifer's back, while Jennifer hoists Carla up. They move back inside the junkyard office.

INT. JUNKYARD OFFICE - NIGHT

The girls lock the door and shut the steel shutters barricading themselves inside the office with chairs.

Jennifer finds a first aid kit and checks Carla's wound --

It's nothing but a flesh wound.

                    JENNIFER
        I'll clean it.

                     CARLA
        Don't worry, it's barely a scratch.

                    JENNIFER
        It'll get infected, if I don't clean it.

Jennifer grabs a bandage wrap and covers Carla's wound.

                     CARLA
        So that's what he does in his spare time.

EXT. JUNKYARD - NIGHT

Russell goes back to his tow truck, puts his hunting rifle away and grabs a high powered automatic machine gun pistol.

He slowly walks to the office knowing that the girls are hiding from him.

                    RUSSELL
        You'll have to do better than that!

INT. JUNKYARD OFFICE - NIGHT

The girls overhears Russell's comments as he toys with them.

RUSSELL (O.S.)

Come on girls, don't be shy. I only want to have fun. It's gets so lonely sometimes... I don't know what to do with myself.

Carla and Jennifer are annoyed at Russell's taunts.

CARLA

You sick fuck!

EXT. JUNKYARD OFFICE - NIGHT

Russell loads his weapon.

RUSSELL
(amused)
Ooh! I love a woman who talks dirty. Can you screw good as well?

Russell laughs sickly.

INT. JUNKYARD OFFICE - NIGHT

Carla and Jennifer speak to each other.

CARLA

And I thought he was cute.

JENNIFER
(sarcastically)
You still like him.

CARLA
(sarcastically)
Yeah right...

JENNIFER
Why would he do something like this?

CARLA
I don't know, probably some homicidal tensions.

JENNIFER
Why do the cute ones have to be the most dangerous?

CARLA
You see how he moves and shoots. He is highly trained.
This guy is really good.

JENNIFER
He's probably just some redneck hunter.

CARLA
He's not a hunter, he moves like a soldier.

JENNIFER
How do you know?

CARLA
Many war veterans, who return home, end up homicidal or mentally insane. I've seen it happen, a dozen
times.

Carla and Jennifer look at the office and see a sign that said: "Authorized
Personal Only: United States Army". Carla recognizes the place.

CARLA

This must be a surplus yard.

JENNIFER

A what?

CARLA

It's where they store weaponry, scrap metal and military wares.

Jennifer asks Carla their next strategy of defense.

JENNIFER

So what do we do now?

BANG! BANG! BANG!

Bullets starts hitting through the windows and thin steel shutters. Just missing the girls.

Jennifer and Carla duck. Carla sees a weapons crate. She goes to it and uses her crowbar to open the wooden crate.

Inside the crate is a stack of hay and on top of that are an old World War 2 Thompson sub-machine gun, and a German MP40 with ammunition.

CARLA

Let's kill his ass. If he wants a war, then we'll give him one.

Carla picks up the gun and loads it.

CARLA

Let see if the guns still works.

JENNIFER

I've never fired a gun before.

CARLA

Learn. Watch me, it's easy. Monkey see, monkey do.

Carla shows Jennifer how to properly load a gun, due to her past training as a military police officer. Carla takes the Thompson while Jennifer takes the MP40.

CARLA

Do you get it?

JENNIFER

Yeah.

CARLA

Good. Get ready.

EXT. JUNKYARD OFFICE - NIGHT

Russell is circling around the small office, whistling and taunting.

RUSSELL

I can't wait forever. Come on out or I'm coming in!

CARLA (O.S.)

Fuck you!

Carla kicks open the door and fires at Russell. Russell takes cover behind junk cars and fires back. Carla and Jennifer escape from the office and try to find a way out of the junkyard.

RUSSELL
(to himself)
Well I'll be damned. Those bitches have guts after all.
Now this is my kind of fun. I love a good fight.

Russell hunts down the women in the junkyard.

EXT. JUNKYARD - NIGHT

Carla and Jennifer travel through the maze of cars as they look for a working vehicle.

CARLA
There has to be a car that works in this place.

They return to the spiked pit where Stacy died, and notice that she is missing.

JENNIFER
Something is not right. Where's Stacy?

CARLA
I don't know, he probably dumped her body somewhere.

JENNIFER
How do you know?

CARLA

I've been overseas during my tour of duty and seen crazy shit like this. Be careful... there's no telling what we'll run into.

At the same time, they are being shot at by Russell. They go around the spike pit to avoid falling in. Then, they run and duck behind a wall of wrecked cars and fire back. The junkyard has become a battleground in a war for survival.

Carla and Jennifer find a jeep as they search for weapons.

JENNIFER

Look.

CARLA

Oh hell yeah.

They find a Panzerfaust rocket launcher covered in the back of the truck bed of an old jeep. However, there is only one small rocket.

Russell pulls out a small whiskey bottle out of his side pocket. He tears a strip from his sleeve to make a rag fuse.

He makes a Molotov cocktail out of the materials and lights it. He throws out the Molotov cocktail at them.

The fire bomb spreads like napalm but misses the jeep. At the same time, the girls duck behind the jeep.

Carla pulls out the rocket launcher and the rocket out of the jeep, while being shot at. She loads the rocket launcher and fires at Russell.

RUSSELL

Oh shit.

Russell dives away from the area and the rocket hits the pile of damaged cars. Scrap metal and debris flies everywhere raining down the sky.

He avoids the falling metallic debris of death by hiding underneath a car. This gives the girls time to escape.

Carla uncovers the jeep and sees a mounted M-60 machine gun.

She hot wires the jeep and tries to start the engine, while Jennifer fires her gun at Russell.

JENNIFER

Come on, Carla, hurry!

CARLA

I'm going as fast as I can!

JENNIFER

Well you'd better go faster!

The jeep drives out of the junkyard.

EXT. HIGHWAY - NIGHT

The jeep drives miles away from the junkyard.

CARLA

We should be in Moreno Valley going this way.

JENNIFER
Thank God.

EXT. JUNKYARD - NIGHT

Russell scrambles out of his makeshift trench and runs back to his tow truck and starts her up. Slamming on the gas pedal he races through the main entrance, chasing after the girls in the jeep on the open highway.

RUSSELL
You can run but you can't hide. Time to die!

Russell laughs like a psychopath as he increases speed gunning it catching up to the girls.

EXT. HIGHWAY - NIGHT

Jennifer looks behind the jeep and see the tow truck on their tail.

JENNIFER
Shit, he's right behind us.

CARLA
What are you waiting for? Shoot him!

Jennifer shoots the truck with her MP40 but runs out of bullets.

JENNIFER
I'm out!

CARLA
Use the M60 in front of you!

Jennifer goes to the M60 machine gun.

INT. TOW TRUCK - NIGHT

Russell continues to fire at them but his gun runs out of ammo as well.

> RUSSELL
> Shit.

EXT. HIGHWAY - NIGHT

Jennifer tries to fire at the truck.

CLICK! CLICK! CLICK!

> CARLA
> It's jammed! It won't fire!

INT. TOW TRUCK - NIGHT

Russell grabs a pack of three grenades from his glove compartment box. He pulls off the ring with his teeth and throws a grenade at the jeep.

EXT. HIGHWAY - NIGHT

Jennifer sees the grenade flying.

> JENNIFER
> Turn!

BOOM!

The jeep swerves and Jennifer falls back on the jeep. Carla grabs Jennifer's arm from falling off the jeep.

JENNIFER
He's using grenades!

Russell throws another grenade.

BOOM!

The jeep swerves again.

Jennifer goes back to the M60, learning from Carla's teaching, fast and on her feet. She gets it to work and starts firing.

BLAM!

Jennifer loses control of the gun which fires in all directions, including at the truck.

INT. TOW TRUCK - NIGHT

Russell ducks while driving as his windshield is blown to pieces, showering him with in glass. The truck pulls back and slows down.

EXT. HIGHWAY - NIGHT

The M60 runs out of ammo.

CLICK! CLICK!

Jennifer tries to fire but nothing happens. She goes back to the front seat. She looks at the back and sees nothing behind them.

JENNIFER

I think we lost him.

The girls are relieved.

CARLA

Thank God! Now let's get outta here before something else happens.

The jeep continues to drive as they see highway lights.

EXT. FREEWAY - NIGHT

They enter an empty but lit freeway that is heading towards Moreno Valley.

CARLA

Finally, some light. Moreno Valley here we come.

JENNIFER

We got to get to the police.

The Jeep is about a mile towards Moreno Valley city limits -only to find that is barricaded off with multiple large cement dividers, emergency lights and traffic cones blocking the exits. A sign reads: "Road Under Construction".

The jeep pulls over.

Jennifer gets out of the vehicle and screams in rage and frustration.

JENNIFER

No! No! No!!!

Carla grabs her Thompson sub-machine gun and fires at the sign destroying it. Until she runs out of ammo.

CARLA

What the fuck?! I hate... this... shit!!!

Carla turns her attention to Jennifer.

CARLA

What the hell did you get us into?! This is all your damn fault!

JENNIFER

My fault, you bitch?! Fuck you!

Carla attacks Jennifer and pins her to the truck bed. She punches the hell out of her.

CARLA

Why do I put up with you?! All you do is whine and bitch!...

Carla grabs Jennifer by the neck to choke the life out of her -- at the same time Jennifer remembers the fighting from home with Bruce.

JENNIFER'S POV

It's Bruce, not Carla, choking her.

BRUCE

Why do I put up with you?! All you do is whine and bitch! Whine and bitch!!! Whine and bitch!!!

Jennifer completely loses it! She grabs the Thompson gun and hits Bruce in the Stomach. Bruce screams in pain and lets go of Jennifer.

Jennifer punches Bruce in the face knocking him on the ground.

She gets up and grabs the machine gun and points it at Bruce ready to kill him.

JENNIFER
Stay away from me, Bruce! Stay away!!!

Bruce is scared out of his mind and speaks to Jennifer.

JENNIFER
I am not a victim anymore!

BRUCE
Jennifer! Don't kill me!

Jennifer, still hallucinating, slightly pulls the trigger.

BRUCE
Please. You don't want to do this.

As much as Jennifer wants to kill him... she can't bring herself to do it.

BRUCE
(begging)
I'm sorry. For everything I've done to you. Let's start over.

Despite the abuse, deep down inside Jennifer loves him.

JENNIFER

I love you.

BRUCE

I love you.

She drops the gun and goes to Bruce and kisses him passionately.

BACK TO SCENE

Carla pushes her off and slaps some sense back into her.

CARLA

Eww! Get off of me!

Jennifer is completely zoned out and does not realize what just happened.

CARLA

What the fuck were you doing to me?

JENNIFER

What just happened?

CARLA

You and I got on each other throats and almost killed each other. Then, you called me Bruce and started making out with me.

Jennifer is confused and shocked.

JENNIFER

I did what?!

CARLA

Yeah, you made out with me. It wasn't that great. No wonder Bruce wants to leave you.

JENNIFER
(disgusted)

Oh my God!

Jennifer realizes what she's done. She coughs and spits.

JENNIFER
(disgusted)

Carla, I'm so sorry. I didn't mean it. I really thought I saw him.

CARLA

You're cracking up, that's what.
I'm sorry too.

Jennifer and Carla are trying to figure out how to get pass the road block.

JENNIFER

Okay enough with the bullshit, let's figure out how are we gonna get out.

Carla looks at the scene.

CARLA

There are no roads, we could go around the barricade. But God knows where it's going to lead us.

JENNIFER

I don't know let's give it a try.

HONK! HONK!

Carla and Jennifer see lights.

> JENNIFER
> (to the truck)
> Hey...Finally, someone is going to help us!

> CARLA
> (to the truck)
> Hey!!!

The girls thinking that they are saved when they get a closer look at the lights... It's the damaged tow truck driving towards the girls.

> CARLA
> Back in the Jeep!

INT. TOW TRUCK - NIGHT

Russell, with cuts on his face, is determined to kill both women more than ever. He has an angry evil grin.

EXT. FREEWAY - NIGHT

Carla and Jennifer quickly dive back into the Jeep, turn around and speed away in the opposite direction.

> CARLA
> He wants to play? Let's play!

Carla drives the jeep toward Russell, playing chicken.

Russell swerves the tow truck to the other side and makes a sharp 180-degree turn.

The jeep drives away and heads back to the highway.

The tow truck chases after the jeep.

EXT. HIGHWAY - NIGHT

Carla and Jennifer drive as far away from Russell as soon as possible. Until the jeep starts to slow down. Carla checks the fuel gauge -- it is near empty.

> JENNIFER
> God damn it! He doesn't know when to quit!

> CARLA
> We are almost out of gas!

> JENNIFER
> What do we do?! He's coming for us.

Carla is going to do the unthinkable.

> CARLA
> We have to go back to the auto shop and get gas.

> JENNIFER
> Are you outta you're fucking mind?! He'll catch up and kill us there!

> CARLA
> It will be no different than killing us walking on foot again. Besides, I got a plan.

Jennifer has to go along with Carla's plan.

Russell's tow truck arrives and accelerates. He rams the jeep.

                    CARLA
    Kill him!

                    JENNIFER
    With what? You wasted your ammo.

Carla didn't realize that until now.

                    CARLA
    Shit! Shit!!!

INT. TOW TRUCK - NIGHT

Out of options, Russell pulls out his Glock pistol from underneath his seat and starts to fire.

BANG! BANG! BANG!

EXT. HIGHWAY - NIGHT

The bullets hits the back left tire of the jeep.

POP!

The jeep swerves out of control. Carla quickly turns the wheel and pushes the brakes.

The jeep flips on its side. The girls fly out of the jeep landing on the grass field separately. The jeep stops flipping.

Jennifer gets up and tries to find Carla.

Russell pulls over and gets out of the tow truck.

Jennifer sees the jeep, thinking Carla is there.

JENNIFER
Carla?! Carla?!

Russell surveys the area seeing the destroyed jeep. He hears Jennifer yelling.

Russell pulls out his third grenade and throws it on the gasoline from the jeep.

Jennifer runs towards the jeep.

BOOM! The jeep explodes.

Jennifer falls. She thinks Carla is dead. She has lost hope, and she's now convinced she is going to die.

Then, Russell arrives and walks very casually and gentlemanly.

RUSSELL
Well, well, well. Look what we got here. You girls have given me a run for my money. I admire that in a woman.

Russell breathes calmly.

                    RUSSELL
        But now... it's time to finish this.

Russell pulls his Glock and aims it at Jennifer who is stunned.

CLICK!

                    RUSSELL
        Click.

Russell laughs -- playfully, but twisted.

                    RUSSELL
        The fun isn't over yet. I'll be generous and give you a
        head start. Move or I'll kill you here and now.

Russell, serious, cocks his gun and fires at her feet.

Jennifer is spooked. She quickly gets up and runs.

                    RUSSELL
        Start running.

Russell goes back to the truck and refills his truck with a one-gallon gasoline can. He is humming casually.

Little does he know -- Carla crawls and slowly gets up and piggy backs on the crane.

Russell finishes refilling his truck and goes back to the driver's seat and drives slowly. He turns on the radio and instrumental country music plays.

INT. TOW TRUCK - NIGHT

Russell lights a baby cigar while driving and listening to country music.

Behind him is Carla, still hanging on the back of the crane and keeping quiet.

EXT. LARGE WEED FIELD - NIGHT

Jennifer, beyond exhaustion, tumbles. She is physically worn to the bone and can barely walk. Then, she sees the auto shop which is still dark.

Suddenly, the lights turn back on as backup generators activate.

Determined, Jennifer continues to travel to the auto shop until she arrives.

EXT. AUTO SHOP - NIGHT

Jennifer re-enters the front porch of the auto shop where Kelly died. She notices that Kelly's body isn't there.

Something is not right. She goes inside the auto shop.

EXT. TOW TRUCK - NIGHT

Carla sees the auto shop about fifty feet away. She jumps off the truck stealthily.

EXT. AUTO SHOP - NIGHT

Russell stops the truck. He gets out of it and opens the garage. A typical car garage.

Carla sneaks in the front porch of the auto shop observing Russell's next move. She is now the hunter and Russell is the hunted. She knocks him out with the monkey wrench.

INT. AUTO SHOP - NIGHT

Jennifer searches for a place to hide and possibly get a drink of water, but she realizes that Russell's truck is there.

INT. OFFICE - NIGHT

Jennifer enters the chop shop office and tries to call the police on the land line phone. But it's still out of service.

Then, a stranger enters the chop shop and enters the office.

Jennifer hides underneath the table. The stranger calls out her name.

                         CARLA
          Jennifer!

Jennifer recognize it Carla.

                         JENNIFER
          Carla!

The two reunite again and hugged.

                         JENNIFER
          Where's Russell?

CARLA

I knocked him out with a monkey wrench. Come on, let's steal his truck and get out of here. He won't be able to take our car since it's out of commission.

Jennifer begins to say something.

JENNIFER

To hell with that, I'm not leaving until that sick fucking pervert is dead.

Carla agrees with Jennifer -- impressed at Jennifer's boldness.

CARLA

Let's do it.

The girls are about to go out to finish the job but...

RUSSELL

Boo!

Russell pops out the doorway spooking Carla and Jennifer. He can barely move due to the monkey wrench hit, and bleeds from the back of his head.

He pulls out his Glock but loses his concentration, dazed.

He points the gun in all directions but falls down dizzy and unconscious.

Carla and Jennifer go to the back door but it's barricaded.

Russell made sure no one escapes.

JENNIFER

Damn it!

CARLA

Let's find another way out.

Carla and Jennifer rush out of the office.

INT. CRAMPED HALLWAY - NIGHT

The girls run into a small but cramped hallway with a wooden floor and try to find another way out of the auto shop.

They open every door but there is nothing but closets fill with junk and cleaning supplies.

JENNIFER

We're trapped!

Carla sees a trap door on the wooden floor.

CARLA

Oh no we're not.

She gets down on her knees and opens the trap door. There is a wooden plank board stairway that goes down into the basement.

CARLA

Let's go down there.

The girls hide in the basement and lock the trap door from inside.

INT. BASEMENT - NIGHT

The basement is pitch black.

> JENNIFER (O.S.)
> It's dark down here...
> (sniffs)
> ...And it stinks, gross.

Jennifer steps on a loose wooden step -- and falls right through an old floorboard. CRACK! CRASH!

She lands in a strange pile. The basement is dark and filled with stench.

It smells like rotten meat.

> JENNIFER
> Ow!

> CARLA (O.S.)
> Are you alright?!

> JENNIFER (O.S.)
> I think I landed on something soft. I can't see anything. Find a light.

Carla search for a light switch. She turns it on. An old rusty light flickers. Carla sees the broken hole where Jennifer landed.

> CARLA
> Jennifer.

Jennifer realizes that she landed on a pile of dead human remains including the corpse of the tow truck driver. There are body parts chopped up and hanging on meat hooks, including Kelly's body parts.

When Jennifer sees what's up, she screams hysterically -Carla throws up.

INT. OFFICE - NIGHT

Russell regains consciousness. He hears Jennifer screaming.

He cocks his gun and heads to the basement.

INT. BASEMENT - NIGHT

Carla jumps down the hole and lands on the pile. She pulls Jennifer out of the pile and covers her mouth to stop her from screaming.

                         CARLA
          Quiet. He'll hear us!

Jennifer stops screaming.

                         CARLA
          Look at this place. Good God!

Jennifer and Carla looks around the grim and gruesome basement. They find a workbench, butcher table, newspaper clippings hanging on the wall. A meat cleaver and various butcher knives lie displayed on the workbench.

They also find Stacy's naked corpse tied up on the butcher table ready to be chopped up.

Jennifer removes Carla's hand from her mouth.

                         JENNIFER
          This guy is one sick fuck. Why would he do this?

CARLA

Check this out.

The girls find a war portrait of him -- a purple heart, a star. "Sgt. Russell James Maddox" is his full name.

CARLA

He was a soldier, like me.

SERIES OF SHOTS

The chop table is loaded with stolen driver's licenses, fake ID's, credit cards, cash, trophies of his victims...

Pictures from his past killings and multiple news clippings: stories of his escape from a mental hospital as a thrill killer.

He was formally arrested for serial killings and for illegal harvesting and selling of victims' organs to make money.

The clippings detail a killing spree from all around the country.

CARLA

So this is why he wanted to hunt us.

They see a picture of Russell and his squad, Russell dressed as a cook, roasting a pig. Pictures show him cutting up the meat. A plaque -- "Best BBQ Cook" -- is also mounted on the wall.

QUICK FLASH

Russell and his team mates relax at a beer blast in rugged terrain, having a BBQ. Russell is dressed in a military cook's getup, cooking and roasting a pig on pit of red hot coals, drinking beer with his friends.

QUICK FLASH

All are laughing and having a good time.

BACK TO SCENE

> CARLA
>
> He's also a butcher.

Jennifer finds invoices, contacts and order forms.

> JENNIFER
>
> Look at this. Order forms. He's not only running an
> auto shop...

> CARLA
>
> ...but a butcher shop too. We are the meat.

She finds a logo on the crate boxes: "Thompsons Meats". It would appear that Russell sells human meat.

> JENNIFER
>
> It's a fucking chop shop! He's the Butcher of Los
> Angeles.

> CARLA
>
> Thompson's meats? I thought they went out of busi-
> ness a while ago.

Jennifer steps on something underneath the workbench. She looks down and finds a small medical refrigerator and a metal safe.

She opens the door, revealing jars of organs with medical orders. And empty jars with the girls' names on them. They were next. She closes the door.

JENNIFER
He's going to butcher us like cattle and have our organs illegally sold.

CARLA
That's why he took Stacy's body -to cut her up on this table.

JENNIFER
Let's take her body somewhere and bury it out of respect.

CARLA
There's no time. We got to figure out how to kill Russell and call the cops.

Jennifer looks at a newspaper article.

JENNIFER
That's not all, look at this.

The newspaper reveals that he killed 20 people in an unemployment office...

FLASHBACK - INT. UNEMPLOYMENT OFFICE - DAY

Russell is waiting in line inside an unemployment office, just after coming home from his tour of duty overseas. Out of a job and coming back to a financially depressed America -no job, no hope and no future.

His mind is already seriously disturbed from seeing the horrors of war while being on the battle front. He is shaking, nerves shot, and zones out. He hears the voices and screams of war. His thoughts form a constant, angry tirade...

> RUSSELL (V.O.)
> What the hell did I think I was doing? Go and risk dying for your country and have a future of opportunity when you come back. Bunch of bullshit.

Behind Russell is in line with several people with families.

> RUSSELL
> I went out there in the Afghanistan Mountains to make a difference for a struggling people...

He is shaking.

> RUSSELL
> And I come back here and I can't even help myself...

He looks at the single mother leaving the room. She is running and crying after being rejected. He is disappointed of what he saw.

> RUSSELL
> I bet that bitch at the main desk is going turn me down, and then I am really going to be fucked. I can't even get a damn job.

Russell remembers the day that he was medically discharged from the military.

INT. MILITARY COURTHOUSE - DAY

Russell stands in from of The military board. They decided that he is medically discharged. They stamped his paper firmly.

INT. UNEMPLOYMENT OFFICE

RUSSELL (V.O.)
Fuck America. Fuck the world. Those corrupt politicians and rich bankers should go volunteer and die to make a desperate living, not us working class folk.

An obese female middle aged desk clerk with glasses and terrible complexion finishes up with a man who is waiting in front of Russell. The man leaves. The clerk then calls out to Russell.

UNEMPLOYMENT DESK CLERK
Next.

Russell approaches the clerk at her desk window.

RUSSELL
I'm here to pick up my VA check.

UNEMPLOYMENT DESK CLERK
Name?

RUSSELL
Russell Maddox. Sergeant at Arms.

UNEMPLOYMENT DESK CLERK
Give me a second.

The clerk scans her computer for Russell's name in the database directory. She finds it.

RUSSELL

Well?

UNEMPLOYMENT DESK CLERK

Sorry Mr. Maddox. There are no benefits for you. Your deadline for your unemployment extension has passed. As for your VA check, the government has reduced its spending. I don't have a check to give to you.

Russell becomes desperate. He badly needs that money.

RUSSELL

Oh come on -- please just give me a little more time. I need that money. I can't get a job.
I've applied for over a thousand jobs and still no one wants to hire me.

UNEMPLOYMENT DESK CLERK

I'm sorry sir. But I can't help you.
Most of the nation is out of work. I'm just a paper pusher. I don't make the federal budgets, the government does.

RUSSELL

Please.

UNEMPLOYMENT DESK CLERK

I'm sorry sir... now come on, the person behind you is waiting to be helped.

A rude truck driver asshole taunts Russell from behind him.

RUDE ASSHOLE
Yeah move on, pal. Join the club!
You're not the only one.

Russell begins to hallucinate as his mind splits from the trauma he can't handle it. He cracks!

He pulls out two loaded dual small 38 snub nose revolvers that are concealed in his shirt sleeves with a set of metal arm mechanisms like in the movie "TAXI DRIVER". He starts shooting up the place, going postal in a violent rage.

RUSSELL
Fuck you all!!!

Russell fires, blasting away the people in line, killing them -- shooting the desk clerk in front of him in the head -people screaming madly, trying to flee from the shooting.

CIVILIAN
Somebody help! Police!

An armed security guard tries to shoot at Russell to kill him, but Russell is too quick and drop kicks the guard in the balls, disabling him. Russell then locks his dual pistols back into his shirt sleeves and grabs the security guard's 9mm pistol. With it, he blows his head clean off at point blank range -- the guard's blood and brains splatter all over Russell's face.

It's the war all over again -- walls and floor soaked in blood. Russell's killing instinct turns right back on as he finishes off the leftover civilians who have not fled, killing the all.

POLICE OFFICER

Freeze! Drop the weapon!

Multiple police arrive on scene and shoot him in the chest and shoulder wounding him.

We flash forward in a beam of light.

INT. LOS ANGELES COUNTY HOSPITAL - DAY

Russell, strapped on a medical gurney, is wheeled to the surgical ward, still bloody and wounded. He is being treated by a team of two doctors and a female nurse.

The medical nurse checks his pulse and monitors his heartbeat on a monitor while putting a breathing tube down his throat so he does not suffocate from loss of oxygen. He is hooked up with rolling IV bag and a separate blood transfusion bag.

DOCTOR #1

We're losing him damn it. Blood pressure crashing. Get the air tube in.

NURSE

Air tube in. He's losing too much blood.

DOCTOR #1

Give the transfusion now.

The nurse opens up the valve on the blood bag while the second doctor presses his wounds down with thick gauze to clot the bleeding.

Russell's body starts to go into shock. He begins to go into convulsions.

DOCTOR #2

He's going into cardiac arrest! Give him one hundred volts.

The nurse preps the defibrillator pads with gel and juices Russell.

NURSE

Clear!

Russell's heartbeat comes back at good pace.

NURSE

Stabilizing.

DOCTOR #2

Good work.

INT. HOSPITAL ROOM - NIGHT

Russell opens up his bloodshot eyes -- only to find himself locked in cell, strapped in a recovery bed. He closes his eyes.

INT. COURTHOUSE - DAY

Russell is chained up in a strait jacket and locked in a holding cart... trussed up like Hannibal Lecter.

The OLD JUDGE, 70s, full of hell's fury, retribution and tribulation, passes heavy judgment. He smashes his gavel on his desk.

OLD JUDGE
(yelling)
Guilty!!! I hereby sentence you to death by means of the gas chamber at the state mental ward, where you will

wait and serve your time until your execution is com-
menced. Case dismissed! And may God have mercy on
your soul.

We hear the sound of the gavel crashing down as we flash into the future.

MONTAGE:

Russell boldly busts out of the mental hospital! Alarms go off!

Russell kills police guards with a stolen police shot gun and pistol.

Russell blasts his way to freedom, fueled with rage and utter hate at the
world for fucking him over...

EXT. OPEN HIGHWAY - NIGHT

Russell speeds off like a thief in the night in a stolen police car, to begin
his nationwide killing spree.

Russell fires his pistol multiple times in the air laughing like a madman
from hell.

Russell goes to the auto shop where he meets the original mechanic. He
shoots him dead and steals his clothes and identity. He sets up his base
of operations.

                    RUSSELL
          Home...

INT. BASEMENT - NIGHT (BACK TO PRESENT)

As the girls stare at the clippings...

JENNIFER
So Russell went mad after the war.
You were right, Carla.

BANG!

Carla is shot in the upper thigh by Russell with a Glock pistol. This time the bullet goes straight through to the bone. Carla can barely move.

CARLA
(in pain)
Fuck!!!!

INT. CRAMPED HALLWAY - NIGHT

Russell shoots into the basement floor with his Glock pistol.

He angrily taunts them.

RUSSELL
So you found my secret hiding spot, eh? You girls wondering why I do what I do.

Russell circles around the trap door.

JENNIFER
We know all about you, now and why you hunt.

RUSSELL
Now you know. When you're screwed by your country, you gotta do whatever it takes to make a living. Even if means crossing the line.

INT. BASEMENT - NIGHT

Jennifer gets pissed as hell.

> JENNIFER
> That means killing innocent people for kicks, you mur-
> derous motherfucker!

INT. CRAMPED HALLWAY - NIGHT

Russell continues to taunt Jennifer.

> RUSSELL
> That's right honey, keep on talking. We can do this all
> damn night. There's no way out.

Russell fires his Glock pistol in the trap door.

INT. BASEMENT - NIGHT

Wood chips fall from the ceiling. The girls lean on the walls to avoid gunfire.

Russell stops firing as he talks.

> RUSSELL (O.S.)
> I remember my tour of duty in Iraq. I still here voices
> in my head.

The voices of war, terror and horror.

Then, the girls find a machete and a butcher knife. Jennifer grabs the
butcher knife while Carla grabs the machete.

RUSSELL

I don't like the voices, but I'm use to it.

Next, they see a wooden storage box that is moving. Someone or something is inside.

JENNIFER

Let's open it.

CARLA

No we don't got time.

The girls didn't bother opening it, as they assume it's another wild animal that Russell captured alive.

INT. CRAMPED HALLWAY - NIGHT

Russell tries break down the trap door by kicking it, but he is unable to open it.

RUSSELL

I tried to be a gentleman, I tried to be kind, but you bitches managed to really piss me off!!! Now you're gonna pay!

Russell continues to kick down the trap door.

INT. BASEMENT - NIGHT

There is dust coming out of ceiling of the basement. The trap door is almost broken through.

JENNIFER
(screaming)
Go Away!!!

RUSSELL (O.S.)
Not a chance!

Russell laughs like a manic, even more wanting to kill them.

CARLA
He's almost in.

JENNIFER
We are going to die.

The girls are out of options.

CARLA
If we attack him when he comes in, he'll shoot us.

JENNIFER
Then, what do we do?

CARLA
We gotta find a way out.

JENNIFER
How?

Russell eavesdrops.

RUSSELL (O.S.)
There is only one way out and that is death!

Carla finds a sheet on her side of the wall. She pulls the sheet down -- it reveals a small window.

CARLA
(whispering)
I got an idea. Give me a boost.

Jennifer goes to Carla and helps her open the window.

RUSSELL (O.S.)
I can do this all day!!!

CARLA
(whispering)
I'll distract him outside.

Jennifer helps Carla get up and crawl through the tight window.

Russell stops kicking the door.

JENNIFER
He stopped.

EXT. AUTO SHOP - NIGHT

Carla crawls out of the window. She survey the scene to make sure Russell isn't outside.

CARLA
(whispering)
He's not here.

Then, Russell pops out and swings his axe. Carla blocks his axe with her machete as the two former soldiers struggle.

CARLA

Jennifer, run!

INT. BASEMENT - NIGHT

Jennifer holds Carla's legs, and tries to pull her back into the basement for safety.

JENNIFER

No! I'm not leaving you!

EXT. AUTO SHOP - NIGHT

Carla and Russell are struggling.

CARLA

Get outta here! Go now!

RUSSELL

(mocking)

That's right piggy, Run, you little cunt!

INT. BASEMENT - NIGHT

Out of options, Jennifer grabs her butcher knife, hops over the hole, unlocks the trap door and exits.

INT. CRAMPED HALLWAY - NIGHT

Jennifer runs away and never looks back.

EXT. AUTO SHOP - NIGHT

Finally, Russell knocks the machete from Carla's hands. He steps on her chest and decapitates her head with an axe.

Carla's body falls down back into the basement with blood splattering everywhere.

Meanwhile, Jennifer heads outside and into the tow truck.

She realizes that there are no keys.

> JENNIFER
>
> Shit! No keys!

THUD!

Carla's severed head falls in front of the broken windshield of the truck.

Jennifer screams.

Russell shows up out of nowhere. He shoots through the tow truck but his gun is empty. He has no more bullets. This gives Jennifer a chance, as she stabs Russell's hand.

Russell drops the axe screaming in agony. But he uses the butt of his Glock and hits her in the forehead, knocking her out.

INT. BASEMENT - _NIGHT_

Jennifer wakes up -- to find herself tied up, mouth gagged, hanging on the meat hanger in the basement. She sees Stacy being carved up by Russell with a meat cleaver.

Russell is singing "Jimmy Crack Corn" with modified lyrics:

RUSSELL
(singing)
"Jimmy crack whore and I don't care...
Jimmy crack whore and I don't care...
Jimmy crack whore and I don't care!!!
I smoked her ass today!!!"

Russell chuckles maniacally.

Jennifer tries to scream but can't. She cries in helplessness.

RUSSELL
I hate to be chauvinistic but... don't you enjoy a good
laugh?

Jennifer is literally crying, helpless.

RUSSELL
Relax, you little bitch. You'll be dead in less than twenty
minutes and then you will join your friends over there.

Russell pulls out the severed heads of Stacy and Carla. He puts them
into jars, right next to Kelly's jarred head.

Jennifer is now having an emotional breakdown -- she's mortified be-
yond comprehension, trapped in the basement with no hope of escape.

Russell drains the blood of the victims and pours it in jars.

RUSSELL
Save N' Shop grocery stores are going to pay me top
dollar for the meat on your friends here.

He mixes the blood and protein power in a blender. He made a blood protein shake and drinks it.

RUSSELL
Mmm...mmm... Delicious.

Russell turns around and looks at her face to face. He has a meat cleaver and a butcher knife. He inspects her like a piece of meat.

RUSSELL
It's a crying shame to cut up such a beautiful body like that. I think you will be more worth to me alive then dead. I know some guys from Thailand who'd pay top dollar for the perfect little sex slave like you.

Jennifer struggles even more as she desperately tries to free herself.

RUSSELL
Now don't look at me that way. A guy has to make a living somehow.

Russell pulls off her gag.

Jennifer breathes heavily, crying.

Russell offers her a blood protein shake at her face.

RUSSELL
Want some?

Jennifer spits on his face.

JENNIFER

I'm a fucking vegan!

Russell takes the spit off his face and licks it. He enjoys it. He grabs a funnel.

RUSSELL

Not anymore.

Russell forces funnel into Jennifer's mouth and pours the blood protein shake. He makes her drink it.

Jennifer vomits all over Russell and coughs!

RUSSELL

You are one stubborn bitch.

JENNIFER

Your sick!

RUSSELL

Any last requests?

JENNIFER

Why bother? You're just going to kill me anyway.

RUSSELL

Because I'm a gentleman.

JENNIFER

Why are you doing this?

RUSSELL

Because I like to.

Russell explains why he hunts humans.

RUSSELL

It's more fun than hunting animals.

RUSSELL

The rules of the game is I become the predator. You
are the prey. If you die, game over. If you live, well...

(PAUSES)

Fuck it! There's NO ESCAPE!!!

Russell laughs. Jennifer continues to cry.

RUSSELL

I have something you want to see.

Russell opens the moving wooden box and reveals his living Male
Victim JONAH, 20, disfigured, anorexic and alive.

RUSSELL

Since you killed Boomer. Meet my other pet, my friend
Jonah. Don't worry about him, he's kinda slow and a
mute.

Russell feeds Jonah. Jonah eats Stacy's dismember breast and drink her
blood Jennifer doesn't speak as she cries.

RUSSELL

Jonah and I use to be war buddies in the POWs in
Afghanistan.

Jonah goes to Jennifer and inspects her body.

RUSSELL

Go on Jonah, check her out. You want to get laid, right back
in Iraqi we use to fuck their women. Now, that was fun.

Jonah nods his head. He attempts to force Jennifer to engage sexual
activity. Jennifer feels humiliated.

JENNIFER

(crying)

Oh God! Please Stop!

Russell pulls out Jennifer's wallet and cell phone. He looks at a picture
of herself and Bruce.

RUSSELL

Look's like your jackass of a husband of yours ain't
gonna save you.

Jonah fondles Jennifer's breast and he kisses it.

RUSSELL

I remember that day. The day when we were captured.

FLASHBACK - EXT. TALIBAN HEADQUARTERS - NIGHT

Russell and Jonah are held prisoner by Taliban Rebels. They are forced
to watch their fellow soldiers burned alive and skinned alive.

RUSSELL (V.O.)

My squad was captured by the enemy. They killed and
tortured my men.

Taliban soldiers grab Jonah and tortured him. They mutilated his face
and cut out his tongue.

JONAH
(begging)
No! Please no!!!

RUSSELL (V.O.)
Then, they made Jonah into a freak and I was forced to watch.

Russell goes insane and kills members of the Taliban.

RUSSELL
Finally, I lost it. I killed as many as I could. Even my fellow men.

A U.S. Rescue team arrives and eliminates the remaining Taliban members, but Russell kills his fellow soldiers in blind rage. Then, he kills innocent men, women and children.

INT. BASEMENT - NIGHT (BACK TO PRESENT)

Russell finishes his story.

RUSSELL
So you see, when you serve your country and later come home knowing your fucked. You lose yourself. The people I killed will always be part of me and I can still hear their screams. It helps me sleep good at night, knowing that I've done my part

(Cont)

RUSSELL
In making the world a more hellish place.

He chuckles wickedly.

Russell enjoys Jonah licking and grouping Jennifer.

> RUSSELL
>
> Do you like it, Jonah?

Jonah drools and nods quickly. He is horny.

> RUSSELL
>
> Every time I hear the screams and voices. I see them
> in the mirror.
> They tell me to kill.

Russell looks at the mirror and sees the people that he killed. He is hallucinating.

Jennifer is thinking with her wits. She remembers Aesop's fable "The Cat and The Mice."

> JENNIFER (V.O.)
>
> Using your wits is sometimes better than trying to
> fight your way out of it.

Jennifer looks around the basement and notices a chainsaw on the ground. She becomes calm.

> JENNIFER
>
> Russell...

> RUSSELL
>
> Yes...

JENNIFER

Will you fuck me?

Russell is surprised.

RUSSELL

Well this is a pleasant surprise...Why should I? When
you kneed my Jimmy...

JENNIFER

My husband hasn't given me good sex for the past year.
If I'm going to be a sex slave, then why don't you try me
to see if I'm any good?

(looking at Jonah)
If you can get him off of me.

Russell wastes no time to take this once in a lifetime opportunity. He
pulls Jonah away from Jennifer and chains him up by the neck arms.

RUSSELL

Jonah, wait your turn. Watch how Russell make's love
to this bitch.

Jonah wants more.

JONAH

More...

He decides to fulfill her request, and unties from her bondage.

RUSSELL

It's been a while since I had some.

Immediately, Jennifer wraps her arms around him and makes out with Russell. Russell takes off his shirt revealing manly six-pack, lean and ripped body. Then, he takes off Jennifer's shirt and bra exposing her breasts. Jonah watches and drools.

JENNIFER

When is the last time you got laid?

RUSSELL

Right after I got back from the war. I went to make out
with a few Filipina hookers and... killed them too.

Next, she gently pins Russell to the ground and climbs on top of him. Ready to make love with him... surrounded by the dead.

JENNIFER

Close your eyes and I will give you a big surprise.

Russell closes his eyes -- he thinks it's a game, which he likes.

RUSSELL

What is this, foreplay?

JENNIFER

You'll see.

RUSSELL

I like it.

Jennifer slowly grabs the chainsaw, gets up and pulls the chain and the engine roars.

Russell opens his eyes and notice something is wrong.

RUSSELL
What the...?!

Russell tries to get up and struggles to grab the chainsaw away from Jennifer.

Jennifer pushes the chainsaw down and slices his groin and pelvis -- blood and gore shoots all over the walls, her face and body.

JENNIFER
How do you like it, bitch?!

RUSSELL
Aaahh! Shit!!!

Jennifer continues to cut him up with the chainsaw -- enjoying it immensely, a sick smile on her face. She is no longer herself. Blood continues to splatter all over her.

Jonah screams, witnessing the horror as he tries to break his chains off.

Jennifer stops and turns her attention to Jonah.

BUZZ!

Jonah begs for mercy, prays and screams.

Jennifer carves his head, groin and lower chest.

JENNIFER
Do you like it?! Do you like it?!!! **Do you like it?!!!**

Jonah dies.

Russell barely alive, crawls down attempting to escape to the surface.

Jennifer finishes Russell off by slicing hid head open like a watermelon and cutting half of Russell's body down. Russell splits open like a banana peel as his brains, guts and organs splash all over the place in a bath of blood on the ground.

Russell is dead.

                    JENNIFER
        Die! Die!!! **<u>Diiiiiie!!!</u>**

Jennifer stops the chainsaw. She screams, totally losing it, her own blood lust revealed, out of control!

Jennifer begins to cry uncontrollably, traumatized that her friends, including her best friend, are all dead.

INT. BATHROOM - _NIGHT_

Jennifer calms down and washes the blood off her chest, face_ _and hair and dries off with a towel. She picks up a black t- shirt from Russell's clothing and looks into the mirror at her face.

JENNIFER'S POV

Russell appears before her in the mirror with ghastly fog and eerie lights.

                    RUSSELL
        I'll always be a part of you now.

                    JENNIFER
    You! You're dead!!! I'm not seeing this. You're not real!

RUSSELL

Yes I am. You see, you and I are more alike than you
realize.

JENNIFER

How?

RUSSELL

We're both fucked up.

JENNIFER

I'll never be like you. You creep.

RUSSELL

Wait awhile. The beast in you is going to break loose
and when it does, you'll remember me and understand
what I did and why I did it. Was it good for you?

BACK TO SCENE

The hallucination ends and Jennifer just sees herself in the mirror now.

INT. OFFICE - NIGHT

Jennifer leaves the restroom and finds a gas barrel back in the auto shop
office. She dumps gasoline all over the place.

She finds a box of matches and a pack of cigarettes.

EXT. CHOP SHOP - NIGHT

Jennifer lights up outside, takes a drag. She then flicks the cigarette
through the open door. Flames shoot up inside.

She runs to the tow truck and hops inside finding the keys underneath the drivers seat. She grabs the jarred heads of her dead friend. She drives away crying and giggles as the Chop Shop blows up...

The terror is over... or is it?

EXT. HIGHWAY - DAY

Jennifer, tired and worn out, drives silently through the morning light on the open highway back to Los Angeles.

Speechless after all the horror from the entire night.

She pulls out a cigarette from her pack and lights up with the matches she still has on her and smokes. She turns on the radio with some soft rock music to calm her down.

EXT. DINER - DAY

She stops off at a diner to have a cup of coffee.

INT. DINER - DAY

Inside the diner, Jennifer sits at the counter sipping her coffee slowly, thinking about the whole night, her dead friends and what she is going to tell Bruce when she gets home. And what about the police?

JENNIFER (V.O.)

What now?

The plasma TV on the wall plays the news. Jennifer watches the news. JAMIE VALENTINE, 30, A female reporter discusses breaking news.

JAMIE
We are live at a crime scene, where exactly at seven
a.m., a local highway patrolman stopped by and noticed
an auto garage on fire. He immediately contacted local
fire fighters, who put out the flaming inferno, discov-
ering a scene of mass murder and mayhem.

The TV shows fire fighters have extinguished the fire. Paramedics remove the bodies.

A POLICE OFFICER, male, 30, is being interviewed by Jamie.

POLICE OFFICER
We found several human bodies were mutilated, hanging on meat hooks in the shop's basement. There were
human heads and organs stuffed in glass jars, as well
as the charred and decapitated bodies of three young
unknown women, presumably raped and murdered.

JAMIE (V.O.)
Also discovered at the site were the freshly killed remains of wanted serial killer and mass murderer Russell
Maddox, known as "The Butcher of Los Angeles" who
was wanted for the deaths of fifty victims including
men, women and even young children.

The TV shows pictures of Russell Maddox, in his uniform and his crim-
inal photo.

JAMIE
The former Iraq & Afghanistan war veteran, who was
unemployed at the time of the start of the murders,
began his killing spree after he became disgruntled,

shooting up an E.D.D. unemployment office, killing twenty people. That was exactly one year ago.

The TV cuts back to the Jamie.

Diner patrons watch Jamie reporting the news.

JAMIE
Now the families of the victims of this madman can rest a little easier with closure, knowing that justice has been served. Not by the police, but by a brave avenging angel out there. This Jamie Valentine, Channel 12 news. Back to the news.

INT. NEWS STATION - DAY

A male reporter, ALEX ROTH, 35, is in the newsroom reporting the latest news.

ALEX
In other news, Congress has passed a bill today that will cut off twenty thousand teaching and administration jobs within the county of Los Angeles, including the most financially depressed areas: East Los Angeles, Watts, Compton, Venice and Inglewood.
Starting today.

The TV screen shows the charts of jobs declining. Teachers and staff members are cleaning out there desks.

INT. DINER - DAY

Jennifer watches the news and thinks.

JENNIFER (V.O.)
Now I understand what he meant.
Society has destroyed the human race.

Jennifer looks into her coffee.

JENNIFER'S POV

She sees Russell's face.

RUSSELL
You see. I told you so. We're all... fucked.

BACK TO SCENE

Jennifer leaves two dollars to pay her coffee. She leaves the diner.

DISSOLVE TO:

EXT. HIGHWAY - NIGHT

Jennifer drives the truck to an open field and abandons it.

EXT. BUS STOP - DAY

Jennifer waits at a bus stop in the Inland Empire. She keeps thinking
to herself.

JENNIFER (V.O.)
Where did we go wrong?

The bus stops and Jennifer gets on. The bus drives away.

DISSOLVE TO:

EXT. EAST LOS ANGELES - NIGHT

After a long journey, the bus drops Jennifer off in East L.A.

INT. APARTMENT - NIGHT

Jennifer comes home and enters her apartment. She brings the jars of the dead friends with her. She charges her dead cell phone and reads the text messages. It's all from Bruce.

The hateful text towards Jennifer said:

"STUPID BITCH WHY DIDN'T YOU ANSWER THE PHONE! I TOLD YOU TO STAY HERE! GO BACK TO YOUR MOTHER! - BRUCE"

Jennifer deletes the text message on the cell phone. She turns on the answering machine and listens to her messages.

BEEP!

                        SCHOOL PRINCIPAL
            This is a message for Jennifer Sanderson. We regret to
            inform you that you have been laid off due to budget
            cut backs starting the end of the semester. We wish you
            all of the best with your future endeavors.

BEEP!

                        DOCTOR #1
            Miss Sanderson, this is the Moreno Valley Hospital
            calling regarding on your mother's health. Please give
            us a call immediately.

She calls the hospital and speaks to either the doctor or her mom on the phone.

JENNIFER (V.O.)
I hope she is okay.

The phone picks up.

JENNIFER
Doctor, it's me. Jennifer Sanderson, I am calling in regards of my mother.

JENNIFER'S MOTHER (V.O.)
Hi honey, how are you?

To much of her surprise.

JENNIFER
Mom?

JENNIFER'S MOTHER
Yes, sweetie. They patched your call to my room.

JENNIFER
I'm okay. They told me about what's happening to you.

JENNIFER'S MOTHER (V.O.)
We'll they told you wrong. The doctors misdiagnosed me. I'll make a full recovery within a year of treatment.

Jennifer is happy.

JENNIFER
Thank God. That's good to hear.

JENNIFER'S MOTHER (V.O.)
They said you were going to be coming to visit me.

JENNIFER
I was... there was an accident on the road. I got a little
sidetracked.

QUICK FLASH

Random images of Jennifer and her friends flash before her eyes in a
series of glimpses of them being killed...

BACK TO SCENE

JENNIFER'S MOTHER (V.O.)
That's alright. At least you tried to come. I'll be fine,
you and Bruce try to hang in there at home.

JENNIFER
I will. Love you mom.

JENNIFER'S MOTHER (V.O.)
Love you too.

JENNIFER
Bye.

She hangs up the phone, breathing in deeply, happy that her mother is
going to live.

Suddenly, she hears a strange noise from the bedroom.

Thinking it's a robber who has broken into the apartment; she goes into
the kitchen and grabs a butcher knife to protect herself.

                    JENNIFER
    Honey... Bruce?

INT. MASTER BEDROOM - NIGHT

Jennifer goes to the master bedroom, only to find her husband in bed
with another woman.

                     BRUCE
    Jennifer? I... I... It's not what you...

Jennifer looks at them coldly as she shakes her head slightly.

                     BRUCE
    Jennifer you look like...

                    JENNIFER
    Honey.

Holding the butcher knife behind her back, Jennifer swings the door
closed and locks it.

                                        CUT TO BLACK.

Russell laughs evilly.

THE END

ABOUT THE AUTHORS

Born Dominic Rocky Daniels, in the city of Anaheim, California in 1984, he was raised in San Gabriel, CA. At a young age his passion has always been in films, animation, and storytelling. He is best known for his dark fantasy / vampire book series: The Damascus Chronicles (Book 1) & The Damascus Chronicles: Denizens of the Night (Book 2), which has won the Amazon Editors Choice Award: Best Books of 2014. Trained in fine art at the age of 10, he decided to go into the entertainment business and become a writer. He is a self-taught author and electronic dance music arranger under his Nega Blast X music production brand. He has a Bachelor Degree of Science in Media Arts and Animation from The Art Institute of California-Los Angeles. In his spare time he reads graphic novels and studies movies, his favorite music is heavy metal.

Trivia: He is a third cousin to the legendary screen actress "Bebe Daniels" who starred in the film 42nd Street.

Website:
www.dominicrdaniels.com

Born as Raynaldo **De** Dios DeLeon II. **Ron** DeLeon is a graduate of The Art Institute of California - Los Angeles with a Bachelor of Science degree in Video and Film Production. He is well trained in the process of professional screenwriting, crew work, video editing, and camera operation. He is best well known for his co-written book *Underground Society*. He has worked for *Cast Iron Productions* as a freelance Casting Editor on the TV show *"Blush"* for *Lifetime Channel* and other show projects. He's worked in production at *Fox Sports West* in Los Angeles, CA and *EBS Entertainment* in Santa Monica, CA.

Currently, Ron is a professional photographer & videographer based in Southern California. In his spare time, he shoots videos as an active video blogger and enjoys watching cult movies.

Website:

deleonpictures.tumblr.com

www.linkedin.com/in/rondeleon

https://www.facebook.com/therondeleon